Double Trouble

KINGFISHER
LONDON & NEW YORK

Text copyright © 2009 by Cathy Hopkins
Cover illustration copyright © 2009 by Monica Laita
Published in the United States by Kingfisher,
175 Fifth Ave., New York, NY 10010
Kingfisher is an imprint of Macmillan Children's Books, London.
All rights reserved.

Distributed in the U.S. by Macmillan, 175 Fifth Ave., New York, NY 10010
Distributed in Canada by H.B. Fenn and Company Ltd., 34 Nixon Road, Bolton, Ontario L7E 1W2

Library of Congress Cataloging-in-Publication data has been applied for.

ISBN: 978-0-7534-6206-5

Kingfisher books are available for special promotions and premiums. For details contact:
Special Markets Department, Macmillan, 175 Fifth Avenue, New York, NY 10010.

For more information, please visit www.kingfisherpublications.com

Printed and Bound in the UK by CPI Mackays, Chatham ME5 8TD
1 3 5 7 9 8 6 4 2

Zodiac Girls

Double Trouble

Cathy Hopkins

KINGFISHER
NEW YORK

Chapter One

Prizes

I have three secrets. Nobody but me knows what they are, not even my twin sister, Lilith. It would be awful if she found out. And not only her; just thinking about how other people might react makes me feel as if tiny butterflies are flapping inside my stomach, trying to get out.

I glanced over at Lilith who was standing next to me at our school assembly. She was my perfect reflection, well, almost—same dark hair, oval face, wide mouth, brown eyes—but if you looked closely you'd see that her forehead is a little higher and that I have a tiny birthmark on the back of my neck. But other than that, it's like looking at myself. It's like I am me but there are two of me.

"Good luck," we whispered to each other at exactly the same time. We often said things in unison. It's a twin thing.

"Same to you," we both whispered back as Mr. Williams sprang onto the stage, stood behind the podium, and took the envelope Miss Regan, our English teacher, had handed him. He made a big fuss of putting his glasses on and then peered over them at the sea of students gathered before him. "And the winner of this semester's poetry competition for seventh grade goes to . . ." He opened the envelope and then paused, in that annoying way that the judges on TV talent shows do when they announce who's still in and who's out. It's an exaggerated pause to build the suspense, and all the contestants have to stand there trying to look as if they're not bothered either way, but you can see them sweating or gritting their teeth. At our house, we yell, "Get *on* with it!" at the TV, but that wouldn't be appropriate here seeing as we're at school and Mr. Williams is the principal. All our teachers have adopted the same manner whenever they announce anything in school these days. It's so boring.

Up front, Mr. Williams smirked at the rest of the staff to the left of the stage and they smirked back, as if acknowledging how cool and modern he was being. All I could think was, *I hope it's me, I hope it's me.* Lilith has won the competition three semesters in a row and, like the Oscars in Hollywood, I figured it was someone else's turn for a change—like mine. Not that I begrudged Lilith winning. How could I? She's my best friend in the world, my sister, my twin. And she writes amazing poetry, like, really intense and dark. It pours out of her like water, or, as my obnoxious older brother, Adam, says, like pus out of a zit. He really is disgusting.

I have to work harder at writing, and this time I'd tried my best to match Lilith. I'd rewritten and rewritten it until it was as good as I felt it could be. I glanced over at Lilith again. She was dressed in our school uniform, which, luckily for us, is black (with a white shirt). I say lucky for us because we're goths. We have been since Christmas of sixth grade, when we went to London, England, and saw a bunch of goths slouch past looking like extras in a Dracula movie. We thought they were the coolest people we'd ever seen, like totally from another era, and we immediately copied the style. Lilith loves it. She says that dressing like a goth is a statement because it is the negation of fashion. She often comes out with stuff like that. God knows what she's talking about sometimes. She's very smart. Personally I like dressing that way because the fingerless black lace gloves and the silver jewelry are so pretty—though obviously we can't wear those at school. I have a great rhinestone cross and Lilith has a ring with a skull on it, and whenever we can get away with it we wear black eyeliner around our eyes to make ourselves look mysterious. Some know-it-alls at our school say goth is long over, but Lilith tells them we dress like we do because we want to, not because we're being dictated to like other losers who are slaves to the latest trend shown in a magazine.

As Mr. Williams continued to scan his audience, Lilith appeared to be relaxed, aside from a tiny vein in her temple that was throbbing—that gave her away. Only I knew that it happened when she was stressed. I bite my nails when I'm anxious. They're bitten down to the quick at the moment. Mom and Dad tried to stop me from biting them by painting some bitter-tasting stuff on them, but I grew to like it. As a last resort, they've scheduled me an appointment with a counselor in the hope that she will get to the root of why I bite them. I have to see her during school vacation, which is next week. Just thinking about someone trying to find out my secrets and make me talk about them only makes me doubly anxious and so I bite my nails even more.

Mr. Williams coughed. "And the winner is . . . [another long pause. Yawn, yawn] Lilith Palumbo."

I put on my best Oscar-loser face (forced smile, clenched jaw) and clapped along with the others. Lilith grinned, squeezed my arm as if to say, sorry you didn't win, then set off for the stage to get her prize. I felt jealous. I couldn't help it. Lilith again. Lilith, Lilith, Lilith. Everything always happens for Lilith. She's often at the top of the class. She's already won the science award and it's only the beginning of October. Now the poetry as well, and she's always picked to be on everyone's team in volleyball and basketball. She's everyone's first choice. I'm like an afterthought: "Oh, and there's Eve, Lilith's twin, better not leave her out." It's like I'm her shadow, hardly a person in my own right. Even though I love her a lot, sometimes it's hard always being in second place. I was born second and have been second ever since. Mom and Dad gave Lilith her name because it means the first woman. (It also means night demon. I found that out when I was looking up our names on the Internet once. I'm saving that juicy bit of information for some day when it comes in handy—like when she brings her first boyfriend home. Tee hee.) Mom and Dad named my brother Adam because he was the first boy and Adam means first man. And they named me Eve because she is sometimes said to be the second woman and they thought they were being clever. Second twin, second woman.

"And I am sure everyone would love to hear our prize winner's poem," said Mr. Williams as Lilith looked coyly at the floor.

"Not really, poetry's so boring," said our friend Mary Stewart from behind me, and I had to suppress a giggle.

Up on the stage, Lilith had gotten out her poem. She coughed to let us all know that she was about to start.

"It's called 'Dark Betrayal,'" she said, and then she began to read in her fake dramatic voice, which always makes me want to fall over laughing. "Around, all around, storm clouds gather. My dread grows as the angry hand of heaven falls against my naked soul. It crushes me and my life's blood drips to the barren land. In pain, I try to run but Death's shadow hovers close. I cry out but my cascade of tears falls upon blind eyes. This is my hell, my fury."

Whamakazoo! Where does she get it from? I wondered in awe as I listened. She's almost thirteen, but what she writes is so grown up and sophisticated. Mom says it's because Lilith is an old soul. I'd written a goth poem, too, with a blood-dripping vampire, a pale Moon, and a tragic heroine, but I knew it was nowhere near as good as Lilith's.

"As if," Mary whispered behind me while Lilith looked modestly at the floor as people clapped. "Your sister needs to cheer up." Instead of joining in the applause, Mary got out her lip-gloss and the air immediately smelled likes strawberries.

Although Mary is friends with both of us, sometimes I think she might be more my friend than Lilith's. Of course, I would never say that to Lilith because she might decide that we can't hang out with Mary anymore. Lilith makes most of the decisions about who we see and what we do, and I always go along with it. That's how it's always been. Although part of me was disappointed that I hadn't won, another part sighed with relief. Lilith isn't used to being in second place like I am.

Chapter Two

Zodiac Girl

After the assembly, Lilith went off to call Mom and Dad and give them the news about her award while I went to the library. It was the seventh graders' time for using the computers, and Mrs. Andrews, our Marge Simpson look-alike librarian, let us surf the Internet and look up what we wanted as long as it was vaguely connected to some schoolwork.

Mary Stewart walked along with me. We made a funny-looking pair because I'm five foot seven and from an Italian background and Mary's a tiny blond, four foot something and a typical WASP. She looks young for her age, a fact that drives her nuts, especially when a bunch of us are trying to get into a PG-13 movie.

The girls in our class are all sizes. Some girls are tall beanstalks, like Ginette Bailey—she's the tallest, at six feet—and then there are the little ones like Mary. Lilith says that Mary is like a small dog in that she makes a lot of noise to make up for her short stature. Whatever. She makes me laugh. I like her. She's funny and irreverent and is the only person I know who stands up to Lilith when she's being bossy.

As we made our way down the hall, we chatted about Lilith and all her achievements.

"What I don't understand," I said as she linked arms with me, "is that seeing as how Lilith and I are twins, both Scorpios with the same horoscope, born on the same day, in the same place, how come our destinies are turning out so different? Like Lilith is a winner and I'm not even a loser. I'm just invisible."

"No you're not—you're just different," said Mary, "and there may be a reason for that."

"Like what? Mom brought the wrong twin home from the hospital?" I joked.

"No. You probably have different rising signs."

"Rising signs? What are they?" I asked.

"Have you ever had your birth chart done?"

"What, like in astrology?"

"Yeah."

"I look at our horoscopes in my *City Girl* magazine each week; it's always the same for both of us. Both of us were born on October twenty-sixth, so we're Scorpios."

"Yeah, but there's more to it than that. My sister Jane is really into it and she explained it to me. To get an accurate birth chart, you need your date of birth, place of birth, and time of birth."

"Why? What difference does that make?"

"A lot," said Mary. "Apparently there's a whole lot more to astrology than your Sun sign, which is like your main sign. The horoscope you read in the paper is usually just about the Sun sign. Like, you're Scorpio, right? And I'm Aquarius. Well, that's only part of it. There are twelve Sun signs. One for roughly each month."

"Yeah. So?"

"So, there are also other planets that affect your chart, like the Moon, Mars, Venus, and so on. I think Jane said that there are ten of them. The Sun changes signs every month, the Moon changes signs every two days—so a whole bunch of Scorpio people will all have their Moons in different places, you know what I mean? If you do your math, in one month, thirty days, that means that the Moon will change signs—"

"About fifteen times."

"Yeah."

"And?"

"And, according to Jane, the Moon in a chart determines how you are emotionally. Like, someone with her Moon in Aries will be smart and sometimes blunt in expressing her emotions because Aries is the sign that leaps before it looks. Someone with her Moon in Pisces would be more sensitive because that's how Pisces is."

"Wow. I never knew that. I wonder where my Moon is. And Lilith's."

"We can find that out, as well as your rising sign."

"So, what's a rising sign, then?"

"That's the part of your chart that determines a lot about your outer personality. Your Sun sign is who you really are on the inside, but your rising sign, or ascendant as it is sometimes known, is how you are perceived by others."

"Like your public face?" I asked as we reached the library. Inside, it smelled like sour-cream-and-chive potato chips and stale air because there weren't any windows that opened and the radiators were usually on full blast. It always stank of whatever anyone had eaten in there last.

"Yeah, and the rising sign changes every two hours."

"Every two hours? Then . . . ohmigod . . . I see, so that's why you're saying that Lilith and I might have different rising signs?"

"It's possible, yeah. Unless you were born at exactly the same time. And you might have the same rising sign if you were born within the same two-hour slot, but say she was born just before one sign changed to the next and you were born just after, then you'd have different rising signs. I think you probably do because you really are so different."

The idea that Lilith and I may be different after all was intriguing. "B-but this is awesome. How do I find out?"

Mary beckoned me over to the computer area, which was behind a glass partition to the right of the main area. "Website. I know the one my sister uses. Do you know your time of birth?"

"I was born twenty minutes after Lilith."

"Let's do it. Jot down your details for me."

I glanced over at the librarian, who was talking to a student from behind her desk. "But will Mrs. Andrews mind? It's not exactly schoolwork."

"Don't worry. We'll fake it if she asks. She rarely does, though."

We found a computer in the corner and I wrote down the details of my and Lilith's birth while Mary logged on to the computer and accessed the website. Moments later, a form asking for personal details appeared. The computer began to play some kind of astral harp floaty music.

"Shhhh," hushed a girl sitting next to us, and she pointed to the notice on the wall asking people to be quiet.

Mary clicked SOUND OFF and the music stopped. I put the paper with our details where she could see it and she began to fill in the form.

"I'll do mine first so you can see how it works," she whispered.

I watched as she filled in answers to the questions and then clicked SUBMIT. Seconds later, a page appeared with a drawing of a circle with lines through it and little squiggly symbols all over it.

"That's my chart," said Mary, and she pointed at the screen. "See how the circle is divided into twelve? Like pieces of a pie? Those are the twelve houses. They represent different aspects of your life—like your career, your goals, your home, stuff like that. And see the little symbols?" I strained to look closer. "Those are the planets. And that tiny circle with the dot in the middle of it is the symbol for the Sun. And this piece of the circle with the two wavy lines across it at the top of the section is the symbol for Aquarius."

"So that means your Sun is in Aquarius?"

"That's it. Now see the little crescent Moon?"

I searched the screen and found a tiny Moon. "Yeah. I see it."

"Well, the Moon is in the piece of the pie with the symbol that looks like a bull's head above it—the symbol for Taurus—so I know my Moon is in Taurus. There's a symbol for each of the planets. I don't know all of them yet. I'm still learning."

"Do the rest of the planets move around every few days or do they all take a month like the Sun?"

Mary shook her head. "All different. Let me see if I can remember. Mmm. The Sun takes thirty days. Moon two days. Mars about six weeks, er . . . Jupiter twelve years, Saturn twenty-eight years—"

"Twenty-eight years!"

"Yeah. I remember that because some of them are really slow moving. Neptune is fourteen years. I forget the others but they're all different."

"Wow. So that must mean a lot of us were born when Saturn was in the same place."

"Exactly, and probably Neptune as well."

"So where's your rising sign?"

"See there?" Mary pointed at the screen. "That squiggle there? That shows what my rising sign is: Gemini. But you don't need to understand any of this, not really. You just type in your details and the computer does it for you, like magic, and then tells you what it means."

"Thank goodness, because I don't think I'd ever get it. It sounds complicated."

"You would get it. It's like anything—you have to learn the rules first and then you can interpret a chart at a glance. My sister's really good at it. I'm still a beginner. I can do Sun signs—that's easy. Anyone can do that. And I can do Moon signs and I can do rising signs. In fact, I think I might be an astrologer when I grow up. Either that or a brain surgeon or a dancer on a cruise ship; I can't decide. So, do you want to do Lilith's or yours first?"

I was about to say do mine first, but then I thought it would be good to know what Lilith's rising sign was first so I'd know immediately if mine was different when we did my chart. "Lilith's," I said, and pointed at her details.

Mary cleared the screen of her chart and typed in Lilith's details. Her chart appeared in seconds.

"Wow," I said. "Impressive. That's so fast. So what's her rising sign?"

Mary scrutinized the screen and then scrolled on to the next page. "Aries," said Mary.

"What does that mean?"

"Well, Aries is the first sign of the Zodiac so—"

"Typical Lilith," I said. "Has to be first in everything."

"Exactly," said Mary. "Aries types like to lead, like to be first in everything, and she has her . . ." she scanned the screen, ". . . Moon in Cancer."

"Let's see if I am Aries rising with Moon in Cancer, too."

Mary cleared the screen again and typed in my details. Once again, a chart appeared. Mary read the screen, then she clapped her hands. "See! There it is. Taurus rising. I knew it! I knew they'd be different."

"Same Moon?"

"Same Moon. Moon in Cancer. That would probably mean that your home is important to you and there's a need for security."

"What does Taurus rising mean?"

"Well, it's a very different sign from Aries, for a start. Aries is a fire sign, Taurus is an earth sign . . . there, read, it tells you."

I leaned over to read the screen and read:

Taurus ascendant. Calm and deliberate, you hate to act hastily. You're very practical, and every effort must count or else you don't want to do it. Patient, persistent, and steady, but very stubborn—you hate to be pushed into anything. You seem confident outwardly, but you repress your inner turmoil. You exude an earthy warmth, charm, and friendliness that draws people to you. You love comfortable surroundings and appreciate the good and beautiful things in life. You can be overindulgent and at times are lazy and difficult to motivate. You are not a self-starter by nature and sometimes need stimuli from others in order to get moving.

As I was reading, the computer began to vibrate.

Mary looked concerned. "Oh no, I hope it isn't going to crash."

It began to shake even more. Suddenly a loud

trumpeting sound burst out. Mary almost leaped out of her chair. "Whoa!"

The girl next to us gave us a dirty look and pointed to the quiet notice again as the trumpet noise began to crescendo.

"I turned it off. I did!" Mary objected, and she went to click on SOUND OFF again, but it was already muted. "I don't understand."

The screen suddenly burst into color—red, orange, and yellow—and a big banner appeared saying, "Congratulations, you are this month's Zodiac Girl."

"Oh great" said Mary. "It's one of those pop-up things." She began frantically pressing buttons. "I'll clear it in a moment."

"Don't shut down. This is for real, Zodiac Giiiiiirrrrrl," came a deep voice from the computer.

The girl next to us was huffing and tutting. Mary looked over at her. "I'm *doing* what I can."

"Eve Palumbo, this is your month," announced another banner, and then a gospel choir began to sing, "Zodiac Girl, you're a star! One month with us and you'll be, be, be, BEEEEEEE who you really AAAAARE."

A few other people in the library had noticed the commotion and looked over at us. Even Mrs. Andrews glanced up from behind her desk. Mary pressed the OFF button and the screen went blank. The noise stopped.

"Phew," she said as the library became quiet again. We got up and made a hasty exit.

"What was that all about?" I asked when we got out into the hall.

Mary shrugged and then giggled. "Dunno, it's never gone crazy like that before, and I've done it for just about everyone I know."

"Must be a pop-up. You know, hundredth person to use the site or something."

"Yeah."

"Yeah."

"Yeah," said Mary again, "but maybe you've won something."

"You think?" I'd never won anything ever in my life. It was always Lilith who walked away with the prizes—but there hadn't been an announcement that *she* was a Zodiac Girl. Could it be that for the first time in my life I, Eve Palumbo, had actually won something? Even if it was only something trivial, I didn't care. It would be a first.

"Worth doing it again," said Mary. "You have a computer at home, don't you?"

I nodded. "Lilith and I share one."

"So do it later."

"I will," I said.

I couldn't wait.

Chapter Three

Moving

"Okay," said Dad after we'd finished supper that evening. (Penne with spinach, tomatoes, peas, and Parmesan. Yum.) "We need to have a family conference. The moving vans will be here over the weekend and the movers will put everything in boxes, so this evening your job is to put anything personal in a small bag that you want to take with us in the car when we go."

He got up from the table and went to put the tea kettle on. I winced when I saw his pants. Yellow cords.

"Dad, where on earth did you get those disgusting pants?" I asked. "They are, like, so last century."

"Found them in the back of my closet."

"I hope you haven't worn them out of the house," I said.

"Why ever not? They do the job. Too many people spend too much time worrying about what they should wear and what's in and what's out. Waste of time, waste of money, waste of resources. Clothes are to cover the body. End of story."

I rolled my eyes. I should have known that I'd get a lecture if I dared to comment on his absence of style. Not that Mom was any better. She was dressed in sweatpants and an old T-shirt. Not that that was unusual either. I don't think she even owns a skirt. Neither of them has a clue when it comes to fashion or style. It's so embarrassing whenever they have to come into school for parent-teacher conferences or school events because both of them look like they got dressed in a hurry in a thrift shop and grabbed the first thing they could find.

"You could afford nice clothes," I said. "There's nothing wrong with looking good."

"As long as it's not dictated by some self-appointed fashion guru who gets paid a fortune to spout their idiotic views," said Adam.

I sighed. Sometimes it was hard living in a house of brainboxes who thought that anything vaguely stylish was flippant or shallow. (Mom and Dad are both academics who work at the local university: Dad is a lecturer in physics, Mom in biology.) Even Lilith supported the anti-fashion philosophy with her argument that our goth style is a statement of rebellion—probably the only reason why Mom and Dad are cool with us dressing this way.

"I should enter you in a makeover show," I said. "So that you get groomed. You could look great if you made an effort."

Mom laughed, but Dad chose to ignore me. It's a shame because they *could* look good. Dad is dark and handsome with a square jaw, which he hides behind a bushy beard, and Mom is pretty with long dark hair that she always shoves in a ponytail, which is forever falling down.

"You can't talk," said Adam. "You and Lilith go around dressed like extras from an Addams Family movie. You can't exactly call that drab black outfit the height of chic."

"It's a . . . um, statement," I said. "Goth never dies, and, anyhow, we were discussing Mom and Dad, not me and Lilith. Given their background and how stylish Italians usually are, they should take more pride in their appearance."

Adam didn't care much about what he wore either, but being a boy, and one who was naturally dark and handsome with no zits, he got away with dressing like a geek. He laughed, got up, and slouched out of the room. He could use a couple of lessons in wearing pants, though; they were virtually falling off his hips and the crotch was almost down to his knees.

"I don't have time to think about things as mundane as clothes," said Dad. "Now then, back to matters in hand. Did you hear me? Tomorrow. Have your personal items packed."

"And he *means* in small bags, no bigger than your

20

school backpacks," said Mom as she began to clear the table. "In fact, use those. The trunk isn't that big and there won't be much room in the backseat with the three of you."

Instinctively, my left hand flew up to my mouth and I began to nibble what was left of my nails. I felt anxious about the move. Not because we were leaving the old house, more because of what had been planned for the new.

Of course, I'd be sad to leave 23 Grebe Street—we'd lived there all my life up until now—but in many ways, the new house was going to be an improvement. More space, a bigger yard, and it wasn't far away—only ten minutes by car, so we could still go to the same school, plus it was closer to the nearby village of Osbury.

No. What was freaking me out was that Mom and Dad thought that since Lilith and I were almost thirteen we might like our own bedrooms for a change.

My first reaction had been to say no way. Lilith and I had always shared. She'd always been there, every morning when I woke up and every evening when we went to sleep, since I was born—and even before that in the womb, although of course I don't remember that. Sometimes I look at Mom's flat tummy and skinny frame and think, *How the heck did I fit in there?* And not just me. Lilith, too. It's astonishing. But my own room for the first time? Would I like it?

I'd been about to say no thanks, and had been sure that Lilith would say the same. But she didn't. She was all for it. Gung ho. Wildly enthusiastic. Which left me with no choice but to go along with it. I didn't want to be seen as a baby or a scaredy cat. And I especially didn't want anyone questioning me about why I still wanted to share in case one of my secrets came out.

"Eve," warned Mom as soon as she saw me biting my nails.

I put my hand down but it was hard. It felt like a magnet being pulled back to my lips.

"And, Lilith," said Dad, "you make sure that you put your prizes and certificates somewhere safe. We don't want any of those getting lost in the move."

Lilith nodded and then we both went up to our room to finish packing. I couldn't help but chew on my nails again as we started going through drawers. I knew that at some point I needed to sneak out to the yard to retrieve the hidden box that held two of my secrets. It was buried behind the shed and I'd been trying to find the right moment all week to get out there alone so I could get it without being seen, but there always seemed to be someone around.

"Do you realize that tonight and tomorrow will be our last nights sharing a room?" asked Lilith as she made a pile of things she wanted to take.

"No. I mean, yes . . . But we'll still have sleepovers

and things, won't we? I mean when friends come over and if we ever feel like sharing."

"Yeah, of course. Like, we'll always be twins, but I'm looking at it as a whole new chapter. I can't wait."

"Neither can I," I said, and put on my Oscar-winning fake smile again. She was looking so genuinely happy about being independent from me that I felt miffed. Had it been so bad sharing a room with me all these years that she couldn't wait to get away at the first opportunity? Well, I was going to let her know that she wasn't the only one who was happy about it. I would see it as a whole new chapter as well. "And not just a new chapter, a new book!"

"It's going to be so cool being able to decorate," said Lilith as she looked at the boring gray-green wallpaper on our walls. It had been there since the people who lived here before us, because although Mom and Dad had always promised to replace it, they had never gotten around to it. "Although I still can't decide whether I want all the walls black for a really dramatic look, or whether to just do the ceiling so it will be like sleeping under a midnight sky."

"I know. It's hard, isn't it?"

"One thing I do know is that I'm going to have a wall for all my prize certificates and poems and stuff. Like a display. You should think about doing the same with your favorite stuff."

"Good idea," I said, although inside I felt totally dismayed. I'd have nothing to put on my wall. Then I remembered the Zodiac Girl thing. Maybe that would give me something to show. "Oh, by the way, did I tell you that I won a prize on the Internet today?"

"Prize. Like what?"

"Um . . . not sure. The computer started like . . . singing and people were looking over and . . ."

"It was probably one of those pop-ups—you know, always trying to get you to click on them so they get your personal information and then rip you off."

"I don't think so. It was on an astrology site."

"Astrology! What were you doing on an astrology site? Not looking at horoscopes again. Honestly, Eve, you know that they're probably made up by some guy in an office somewhere who knows nothing about the stars. And Dad says that astrology is trash for people who have nothing better to do with their time."

"He says that about just about everything. And Mary said that horoscopes in the paper are very general, but if you do them properly then it's like a real science."

"Mary. What does she know?"

"Quite a lot, for your information. Like, did you know that we have different ascendants?"

Lilith stifled a yawn. She hated that I (or Mary) might know anything that she didn't, but I quickly filled her in on everything I'd learned that day anyhow. After I'd finished, she still looked dubious.

"Okay, then show me," she said.

I got the web address out of my backpack, turned on the computer, and went through the steps that Mary had done earlier that day.

"I'll do yours first to show you how it works," I said, and I prayed that the computer hadn't reprogrammed itself in the afternoon so that now Lilith was the Zodiac Girl. That would be just my rotten luck, the story of my life. Moments later, her chart appeared and I explained what Mary had told me.

"Okay," she said, still doing her best to look unimpressed. "So print it out and I'll read it properly."

I clicked PRINT and seconds later she had it in her hand.

"Hm, Scorpio. That's us, isn't it?" she said as she read the printout. "Intense, complex, secretive. Brood a lot. Unforgiving. Pff. We don't sound like much fun, do we? Can lash out. Intuitive. Oh, this part's okay. Loves mysteries and the supernatural. That's true. A good detective. Yeah. Willful, powerful, passionate, and loyal."

"Yeah, but read about your ascendant, Aries," I said, "because that's you, too. We are made up of lots of different aspects and both of our charts are the same except for the part about rising signs. Mary said it explains a lot about why we are so different."

Lilith put the printout down. "You don't honestly believe this stuff, do you?"

"I . . . I am keeping an open mind," I said. I knew she couldn't argue with that. Mom and Dad were both always telling us how important it was to keep an open mind and not jump to conclusions. Tee hee. That shut her up.

"Okay, so do yours, then," she said.

I typed in my details and my chart appeared. I was pointing to the part that said I had a Taurus ascendant when the computer began to shake in the same way as it had back in the library.

And then came the trumpet sound and the gospel singers. "Zodiac Girl, you're a star! One month with us, and you'll be, be, be, BEEEEEE who you really AAAAARE."

Lilith made a scornful face. "Ohmigod, how totally juvenile. So, Zodiac Girl, what do you get? A pen? A badge? A widdle tiara with the words *Zodiac Girl* on it?"

"I don't know," I said as I scanned the screen. There was no evidence of any prize or anything asking for my mailing address so a prize could be sent. As I scrutinized the page the singing faded and the screen went back to simply the text explaining my chart.

Lilith immediately picked up on my disappointment and put her hand on my shoulder. "Oh well," she said. "Sorry I made fun of it, but it was clearly just a silly promo. I didn't want you to feel let down. Don't let it get to you."

"I won't," I said. But I *did* feel let down. I had really thought that for once something good might have been happening just for me. But I was wrong.

After we'd packed a few things into our backpacks ready to take to the new house, we went down to watch television.

"Anyone want a hot chocolate?" I asked.

Adam looked up from where he was draped on the sofa. "Yeah, of course, but . . . what's the catch?"

"No catch. Just, I want one so I might as well make one for everyone."

"Me, too, then," said Lilith, and she moved Adam's legs aside and settled down on the other end of the sofa.

I checked to see what Mom and Dad were doing and found them down in the basement. "You all right down there?" I called.

"Just packing up the good wines," Dad called back. *That's a joke*, I thought. Dad's wine collection was his pride and joy. It wasn't an expensive collection like Mary's dad's; he gets his wine from vineyards in France. My dad makes his own. He likes to experiment with flavors and makes rhubarb wine, orange wine, grapefruit-and-mint wine. Lilith and I tasted the elderberry-and-gooseberry one once. It was awesomely awful and I got a stomachache afterward. We nicknamed it Krudo, which Mom thinks is funny but Dad doesn't. He takes his wine-making very seriously.

Once I knew that everyone was occupied, I went through the kitchen, found the flashlight on the back porch, and snuck out into the backyard. It was cold outside and the air smelled of damp and woodsmoke. My heart was beating fast at the thought of anyone coming out and seeing me, so I quickly raced over to the shed area. Once there I shined the flashlight down to the back where the ground was paved with stone. Two slabs down was the loose one. I lifted it out of the way and reached behind and under the shed where there was a small gap. I dug with my hands and pulled out a bit of loose soil, removed a couple of bricks that I'd placed to mark the spot, and then dug a little more. It only took a few minutes as I hadn't buried the box very deeply

I felt around in the soil until I found the hard surface of the tin and then I pulled. It came out easily. I hid it under my sweater and ran back inside. I quickly checked in the living room to make sure Adam and Lilith were still absorbed.

"Won't be a mo with the drinks," I said.

"Yeah, hurry up, slave," said Adam.

I ran upstairs and was about to shove the box into my backpack ready for the move when I realized something. Given that my secret tin contained only papers that would shock Lilith if she saw them, it felt heavier than normal. I'd had this box since I was ten years old and used it to collect pages from magazines or newspapers that I liked but didn't want to have to explain to any of my family. Also in there were my poems that I'd never shown anyone. I opened the lid and looked inside. My heart skipped a beat. There were two packages wrapped in red tissue paper. One small, one medium size. I hadn't put them there. *Someone knows about my secret place!* I thought as I heard footsteps on the stairs. *Oh no.* I knelt down and quickly pushed the packages under the bed. As I did, I caught a glimpse of a label on the side of the medium-size package. *To the Zodiac Girl*, it said.

Seconds later, Mom's face appeared at the door. "What are you doing, hon?" she asked. "I thought you and Lilith had finished packing."

"Few last things," I said, trying to look as innocent as I could.

Mom stared at my face. "You okay? You look a bit flushed." She came over and put her palm on my forehead. "You're not coming down with anything?"

I shook my head, got up, and sat on the bed. "Nope, fine."

And then Lilith appeared. "Hey. What happened to my hot chocolate?"

"Oh, yeah! I . . . er . . . remembered something I had to pack. I'll do it now."

Lilith sighed heavily. "There's nothing on TV

tonight. Adam's gone out to get a DVD so I'm going to read for a while."

Whamakazoo! I thought as she switched her bedside light on and then settled down on her bed, *that was a narrow escape!* When I stood up and went to make Lilith's drink, my mind was reeling with questions. *What's in the packages? Who put them there? And, worst of all, have they read any of my poems and discovered one of my awful dark secrets?*

Chapter Four

Spook Night

"Eve, *stop* biting your nails. I can hear you even over the movie soundtrack," said Lilith without even looking at me.

Adam swiveled around, stuck his fingers in his mouth, and started making slurpy noises. "Yum yum," he mocked as he sucked on his nails. "I like to eat leetle girls' fingers. I chew them right down to the bone and then I crunch them to a paste and use it as a facial cream to keep my skin silky smooth. Isn't that right, Eve? You are secretly a blood-sucking vampire and your favorite type of blood is your own? Woo hoo HOOOOO."

"Yeah, ha ha, most amusing," I said, but I did take my fingers away from my mouth as the credits of the movie began to play on the TV in the corner of the room. We had just watched the DVD that he'd gotten from the rental store. Of course it had been a horror movie. *Headless Zombies Hit Miami*, it had been called. *One of these days, very, very soon*, I thought, *I have to tell them my secrets*. I have to because I can't go on like this, plus I'm running out of nails to chew on. In fact, if someone were to market stick-on edible nails that nail-biters like me could buy, they'd make a fortune.

Adam reached for the remote and was about to turn the TV off when a commercial for a house makeover program came on.

"Don't turn it off just yet," said Lilith. "I love the guest host who's been on the past few weeks. He's a goth prince. We both love him, don't we, Eve?"

I nodded as an image of the guest host appeared. Every few months, a new interior designer was invited to come on the show with their ideas. The new guy's celebrity name was the Transformer and Lilith had a crush on him; she had a poster of him on the wall above her bed. Tall with shoulder-length dark hair that he wore tied back in a ponytail, he was every goth girl's dream.

"He's old enough to be your father," said Adam. "How can you like him?"

"Better than some skinny boy-band loser with zits," said Lilith. "The Transformer is so charismatic, like he's a wise old soul and knows stuff."

"Pff," said Adam. "He looks more like he's been dug up from somewhere. He needs a bit of sun or something."

The trailer for the program played with images of the Transformer holding various model poses in front of the buildings where he'd done his makeovers.

Standing behind him in all the shots were his two strange-looking assistants, a severe-looking blond girl and a stocky man with a shaved head. They looked intense. Then the screen images changed and went on to the usual commercials for detergent, breakfast cereal, and baby wipes.

"Okay, you can turn it off now," Lilith ordered.

"Thank you, Your Majesty," said Adam. He clicked the TV off and then sprang to his feet. "So, my leetle seesters, how about, seeing as we move on Sunday, we go next door for one last time?"

Oh, noooo, I thought as panic gripped me. I was about to blurt out one of my secrets right there and then, but Lilith was also up on her feet.

"Oh yes, let's. We have to for old time's sake, right, Eve? And we might not get a chance tomorrow night when most of the work has been done and Mom and Dad are ready to go. Let's get our coats, and, Adam, you make sure Mom and Dad are out of the way. Come on, Eve."

"Yeah, but we're not moving that far away. I mean, we could go any time."

"Nah," said Lilith. "Won't be the same. We won't be able to sneak back through our secret passage through the trees in our yard ever again. I think we should go tonight and do a goodbye ritual."

"Me, too," said Adam. "You scared, widdle Eve?

Did the scare-wee movie fwighten woo?"

"Pff, that wasn't scary at all. Takes more than a few headless bodies to frighten me. So, yeah, let's go, for old time's sake. But, er . . . what about Mom and Dad? They might hear us."

Adam quickly snuck upstairs and then returned moments later. "Sleeping like babies," he said. "Or, should I say, a very loud-snoring baby in Dad's case."

We found our coats and headed for the back porch.

"Where's the flashlight?" asked Lilith as she looked around. "Someone's moved it."

I felt it in my pocket from when I'd been out earlier.

"Maybe Dad packed it," said Adam. "We don't need it. Be more fun if it's totally dark." He looked out the porch window at the sky. "And there are lots of clouds so it will be pitch black out there."

There was no way I was going next door without the flashlight. No way. I turned around and as Adam unlocked the back door I pretended I had seen it on a shelf to my right.

"Nope, there it is," I said, and quickly pulled it out of my pocket so they could see it in my hand.

"I don't think we need it," said Adam.

"Just in case," I said, and Lilith nodded in agreement.

"Although if we're going to do a goodbye ritual, it would be better if we had a candle," she said. "I'll just get one from under the kitchen sink, unless they've been packed up." She went to rummage around in the cupboard and emerged with a candle and a box of matches that she stuffed into her pocket.

We crept along the path in the yard, over to the right behind the hedges, and then Adam climbed over the knee-high picket fence and through a gap between the row of pine trees. It was easy to do because we'd been this way so many times.

Moments later, we were next door. Next door in the cemetery. A slender moonbeam shone out from behind the clouds and briefly illuminated rows of silent graves. Our eyes soon adjusted to the near darkness. Angels stood out against the night, their wings spread as if protecting whoever lay beneath the ground. At the top of other graves were simple headstones with engravings telling who they belonged to. A few vases with flowers could be seen, some fresh as if newly placed, others dried up, having been left unattended for weeks. In the background, the skeletons of trees, some stripped of their autumn leaves, were silhouetted against the dark sky. I shuddered with the cold.

"Okay, Evebud?" asked Lilith.

I nodded. "Yeah. Why wouldn't I be? And don't call me Evebud." My family sometimes calls me "Evebud" and even "Evepud" or "Evepuddle," which I find *very* annoying. No one ever messes around with their names.

"Just asking," said Lilith. "No need to be snippy."

"I wasn't being snippy. And I'm fine." Actually I wasn't. And that was one of my secrets. I was terrified, as I had been on pretty much each and every occasion that we'd ever been to the cemetery, starting with the first time when we were eight. It was Lilith and Adam's favorite place and they loved to sit on a grave and tell ghost stories. Sometimes they even dressed up as ghosts and ghouls, especially at Halloween.

All our friends had been invited at various times when they'd been staying for sleepovers—seemed most people liked to be spooked—and it soon became the Palumbo party trick: scaring the living daylights out of our friends. I'd never liked it. Not once. All I'd gotten out of it was a nail-biting habit and a bunch of neuroses. Of course, I had realized very fast that I could never let on how scared I was or how I truly hated going there. I'd have been left out of everything. And I'd have been laughed at. As time went on, Lilith had used her experiences there to feed her poetry and her image as teen goth queen, and Adam had used his time there to win new friends by demonstrating how brave he was, how spine-chillingly scary he could be, and how there wasn't a dare he wouldn't do or scary place he wouldn't venture into—aside from the crypt at the far end of the cemetery. Even Adam wasn't stupid enough to go in there. It was rumored that six children in the eighteenth century had gotten locked in there on Halloween and the next morning all that had been found were their clothes and scratches on the door where they'd tried to get out. Their remains were never found. The story was that if anyone was in there on Halloween at the stroke of midnight, their bones would be turned to dust and scattered over the graveyard. There were six graves next to the crypt that were said to have been put there as a reminder of the lost children. It gave me the shivers walking past in the daytime, never mind at night.

Suddenly Adam leaped out from behind a tree. Lilith shrieked and laughed while I fell back against a gravestone and grazed my arm. I so wished that he wouldn't do that. I found my balance and took a deep breath. Maybe now was the time to tell them about my secret fear, as part of our goodbye-to-the-cemetery ritual. To tell them that our visits to the cemetery had left me with a fear of the dark, a hatred of horror films, and an aversion to cemeteries and had given me nightmares.

I was so glad we were moving to a place with houses on either side. Houses that Lilith and Adam hoped were haunted. Houses I hoped hosted only living souls. But the move brought for me a fresh fear: my own room. Seeing as I was scared of the dark, the idea held little to look forward to. It had been okay as long as I shared with Lilith—like her presence would protect me and make me feel brave. In the new house, I'd be on my own and I was dreading it. It was time to come out of the closet and admit that I, second-in-command to Lilith the goth queen, actually hated the dark. I took a deep breath to summon up the nerve.

"Actually, guys, I have something to tell you," I started.

"Great. A new ghost story," said Adam, and he stood next to a statue of an angel that hovered above the grave of someone named Eric Barrington, who died in his sleep in 1986.

For the second time that night, my courage failed me and I blurted out a joke that Mary had told me yesterday. "What kind of ghost haunts a hen house?"

"Don't know," chorused Adam and Lilith.

"A poultry geist."

Lilith and Adam groaned.

"That's not even funny," said Lilith.

"Don't you have anything scary to tell us?" said Adam. "It's always Lilith and I who come up with the good mysteries."

"Only that she's a . . . what was it, Eve? Oh yeah, a Zodiac Girl," said Lilith.

"What's that?" asked Adam.

"Oh, nothing," I said. "Just some stupid pop-up on the computer."

Just at that moment, I saw something move behind

Adam's shoulder, something in the trees. I looked over. Not something. Someone. A figure in a black cloak. "Ohmigod!" I screamed and pointed. "Over there. There's someone there."

Lilith and Adam almost jumped out of their skin.

"What? Who? What did you see, Eve?" asked Adam.

I felt like I could hardly breath. "A . . . a figure, a tall . . . I think it was a man. Adam, *no*."

Adam had raced over in the direction of the trees. "Come out, come out, whoever you are," he called, then looked around. "No one here."

Lilith linked my arm in hers. "Nice one, Eve. You really had us going for a moment there. That scream sounded totally genuine."

"But I did see someone, I *did*."

"Yeah, yeah," she said as Adam came back to join us.

"No one there, kiddo," he said.

My heart was beating like mad. "But you have to believe me. I know what I saw and I didn't imagine it. Let's go home." I set off toward the gap in the pine trees, but Adam pulled me back.

"You can drop the act now," said Adam. "You had us going for a while with that five-star scream and we know what you were up to—trying to make up for the lack of a good story. See, what we'd really like from you is a good scary story like the ones that Lilith and I come

up with, my little—what was it you called her Lilith?—
Zodiac . . ."

"Zodiac Girl," said Lilith. "And apparently we both
have different rising signs or whatever. Eve has been
looking at astrological sites again."

I glanced back over at the trees, but all was still. Not
a sound, not a movement. All the same, I felt anxious
to get home. Adam crossed his eyes and put the
flashlight under his chin so that his face lit up like a
ghoul. "Eve Palumbo. Astrology is for morons, for
people with no brains, so that must mean that you
have no brain, which means that someone has eaten it.
Someone came in through the window one night and
scooped your brain out through your ear."

"Or maybe they sucked it out with a straw," added
Lilith. "Through your eyeball."

"Ergh," I said. "Will you cut it out? That is so
disgusting, and astrology isn't for morons. Lots of
people with brains use it."

Adam turned the flashlight on and off so that his
scary face appeared and then disappeared. "Give me
one good argument to convince me about something to
do with astrology."

"Okay. I . . ." I looked up at the sky where the
moonlight was struggling to come through the clouds.
A cloud drifted over and suddenly I could see the clear
crescent Moon. "Okay, look at the Moon." Lilith and

Adam looked up. "We all know the Moon affects the sea, affects the tides, right?"

"Yeah," said Adam. "Everybody knows that."

"And we know the Sun affects our planet in lots of ways: gives us light, heat, affects the plants—"

"Et cetera, et cetera," said Lilith as if she was bored.

"Okay, so that's just two planets that we know are affecting us. In astrology there are ten. I don't know exactly what they do, but they're all in different positions in the sky, right? Some closer to Earth, some farther away. And if the Moon can affect the sea and the Sun can affect the plants, then why can't they affect human beings, too?"

"What are you trying to say, Evepud?" asked Adam. "Because I can tell you that so far I'm not convinced."

"I'm trying to say that there might be elements out in the sky that affect us, too, seeing as we are living things on this planet. It's like one giant computer programmer up there—all the different elements around when you are born determine certain things about you. Where the ten planets are in the sky and what angle the Earth is on its axis create something totally unique in you."

Lilith nodded. "I think I'm with you."

"Which is why by the time I was born twenty minutes later than Lilith, the alignment of the planets up in the sky was very slightly different from when

Lilith was born. Because Earth had rotated a bit the planets were all at very slightly different angles."

Adam nodded. "Maybe you have something there. It might explain why she's such a bossy nuisance and you're not." Then he laughed. "But, then again, you might be talking total nonsense."

To Lilith's right, I saw a movement out of the corner of my eye. I glanced over behind her and I swear I saw a shadow moving through the trees. It was so dark it was hard to see exactly.

"Behind you, Adam," I gasped. "In the trees! I'm sure there's someone there."

Adam didn't even bother turning around. "Yeah, yeah, you got us the first time. At least try something new."

"But I—"

"Yeah," said Lilith. "Like, bo-oring."

"Lilith, you know when I am telling the truth; you know that you do."

Lilith looked deep into my eyes for a few seconds. "Okay. I think you are, but Adam says there's no one there and I think he's telling the truth, too, and, well, you know how you start imagining that you're seeing things when you're tired. I think you're just tired. It's late . . ."

I'd had enough. I wanted to get out of that cemetery as fast as possible. "Okay," I said, and I tugged on Lilith to go back to the gap in the pine trees. "Okay, maybe that's it. And, fine, so I can't come up with a good scary story tonight and I can't explain astrology either, but there's something else I can't explain. A *real* mystery . . ." I made my voice go into a scary whisper ". . . and it's at home under my bed at this very minute."

"What? An old sock and a smelly sneaker?" asked Adam. "No mystery there."

"No really. I . . ." I hesitated for a moment while I asked myself how I was going to explain the tin with my secret things in it and the place that I'd hidden it for years. Then I realized that it didn't matter if they knew the hiding place because we were moving and I wouldn't need it anymore. If I could get up to the room fast enough, I could pull the secret papers out and hide them under my mattress and only show them the mystery packages.

"So what's under your bed, then?" asked Lilith. "A body?"

"Course not. Look, I wasn't ever going to tell you this, but I had a place in the backyard where I used to hide things. An old tin box . . ."

Lilith looked surprised. "You had a hiding place that you didn't tell me about?"

"You don't know everything about my life, you know."

She looked miffed. "Apparently not. So what did you keep in there?"

"Oh, nothing important. Things from when I was a kid, like old stones or seashells that we'd collected on vacation, that sort of thing."

"But why didn't you tell me?" asked Lilith.

"Dunno. I just wanted . . . dunno. Anyhow, I hadn't put anything in there for ages," I lied. "But I went to dig it up because it was a nice old tin. I got it one Christmas with chocolates in it. It had doves on it. You got a similar one, Lilith; mine was red and yours was green. I think you threw yours out."

Adam looked bored. "And what? You dug it up and there's a couple of moldy old chocolates in it and a dead rat?"

"No. I dug it up and there were two packages in it."

"That you left there," Lilith prompted.

"No. That I *hadn't* left there."

That got their attention.

"No way. You're making it up," said Adam.

"No, I'm not."

"So what was in the packages?" he asked.

"I don't know yet."

"Why didn't you open them?"

"I, er . . ." Once again I hesitated because I didn't want to tell them the whole truth and a part of me wished I hadn't opened my mouth at all, but I was desperate to get them out of the cemetery. "Mom came in and I didn't want her to see."

"She probably put them there," said Adam, and Lilith nodded in agreement.

"No. I don't think she did. She didn't know about my hiding place. And both packages were wrapped in red paper. Nicely wrapped. And we all know Mom doesn't do nice wrapping. She shoves things in boxes and slaps some Scotch tape on them."

Lilith nodded. "That's true. So what did they look like?"

"Like they were wrapped at the mall. Nicely . . . but what was even more interesting was that one had a label that said 'To the Zodiac Girl.'"

Adam burst out laughing and clapped slowly. "Oh, good effort, Eve. Not very scary, but nice try."

"No, I'm telling the truth."

"Okay," said Adam. "When was the last time you put anything in your widdle tin, widdle Zodiac Girl?"

"Ages ago," I lied. Actually it had been a few weeks ago, but I wasn't going to tell them that in case they found my papers.

"Only one way to find out if she's telling the truth," said Lilith.

"I guess," said Adam. "Let's go check it out."

At last, they began to move toward the gap in the pine trees.

"Goodbye, cemetery," Adam called out.

"Shush," I said. "You'll wake Mom and Dad."

"As well as the dead," said Lilith with a laugh. "But don't you think we ought to do a ritual with the candle and everything? Do it properly?"

"No. Let's go back and, er . . . come back on a special night. Like Halloween night or something. That's only at the end of the month, so not long."

"I suppose it is getting late," said Lilith, "and we have to get up early in the morning."

"Goodbye, ghosts and ghouls, goodnight, all you who rest here," said Adam in a loud whisper.

"May your tormented souls find peace," said Lilith as I pulled her along.

When it was my turn to crawl through the bushes, I glanced back to make sure no one was behind us or following us. And, once again, I swear I saw someone. Just for a second as the Moon came out from behind a cloud and illuminated a gravestone, I glimpsed a tall, dark man in a cloak. For a split second, the moonlight caught the whites of his eyes as he turned and I was certain he was looking straight at me. I pushed through the trees, misplaced my hand and almost fell on my face, but I couldn't resist turning around one last time. The man was gone and all I saw was a beam of moonlight, like an empty spotlight falling on the grave where he'd stood only seconds before.

Chapter Five

P. J.?

"You go into the living room," I said, once we were back in the kitchen, "and I'll go get my box."

"Nah, we'll come with you. You might cheat," said Adam.

I rolled my eyes. "Like I'm going to be able to wrap two packages in five seconds. Give me a break. And why would I want to cheat? Trust me, Adam, I just don't want to wake Mom or Dad."

"Yeah," said Lilith. "She either has these packages or she doesn't."

"Exactly," I said, and I ran out of the kitchen and up the stairs before they could change their minds again. Up in my room, I reached under the bed, grabbed the tin, pulled the wad of secret papers out and stuffed it in my backpack, then went back down the stairs, taking two at a time. Lilith and Adam were waiting in the living room.

"Here you are," I said, and handed Lilith the tin.

She looked down at it, opened the lid, and there were

the two red packages. She lifted them out and was about to open them when Adam stopped her hand.

"Actually, they're Eve's packages. She should open them."

For a brief second, annoyance flashed across Lilith's face, but she soon pushed it away. "Yeah, course," she said, and put the presents back in the tin and handed it to me.

"I don't mind, Lilith," I said. I felt bad that she hadn't gotten anything to open. Up until now, there had always been presents for both of us. Nobody ever gave one of us something without including the other— besides prizes at school, that is.

"Whatever," said Lilith. "Like I care." But I knew she did. We often knew what the other was thinking or feeling.

"I tell you what: you open one, I'll open the other," I said, and I handed her the smaller package. I could see that despite trying to act like she didn't care, like me she couldn't wait to rip the paper off and see what was inside.

"Oh, come on, you two," said Adam, "this is getting boring. On the count of three, open the packages. One . . . two . . . three . . ."

We ripped.

"Oh," I gasped when I saw what was inside mine. It was a tiny cell phone, totally exquisite, stylish, and goth. It was blood red with a black opal stone. "It's gorgeous."

Lilith glanced over and I saw admiration flare in her eyes, but like the annoyance only moments ago she squashed it down. "Yeah, but does it work?"

I pressed a few buttons and then held it up to my ear. "Not sure." I looked in the package to see if there was an instruction book, but I couldn't see one. I was about to chuck the wrapping paper in the trash when a little gift tag floated out.

Adam grabbed it and read it. "Zodiac Girl, I'll call you soon. Yours truly, P. J."

I felt a shiver go down my spine. This wasn't any story made up by Lilith or Adam. This was really happening. "P. J.? P. J. who?" I asked.

Adam shrugged. "Secret admirer? Stalker? Ax murderer? Could be anyone. What's in the other package?"

Lilith looked down. She had unwrapped a small box, the type that usually held jewelry, but she hadn't opened it yet.

"Go on," urged Adam.

She opened the box and a lovely woody scent filled the air. Inside was a silver chain with a charm. She held it up. The charm was in the form of a tiny scorpion and, like the phone, it was exquisitely made. I could see that Lilith wanted it and it seemed only fair to me that we share the gifts. One for her, one for me. In fact, I was starting to feel spooked by the whole thing, whereas I could tell that Adam and Lilith were totally enthralled.

"You can keep that if you like," I said. "And be a Zodiac Girl, too. It's not really my thing."

Lilith smiled, but then she noticed that inside was a small tag like the one with the phone. She picked it up and read. "For Eve Palumbo, this month's Zodiac Girl." She handed the charm to me. "I can't keep it. Whoever sent it clearly meant it for you."

"No. They probably didn't realize that we're twins. No, really, you keep it," I said, and tried to hand it back to her.

"No. I don't want it," she said, pushing my hand away. "I can get my own like that any time down at the market."

But we both knew that she couldn't. The one I held was like nothing I had ever seen at the market or in the stores that sold goth accessories, plus it looked very expensive.

"So you're saying that these things just arrived in your tin that had been buried in the backyard for ages and that you didn't put them there?" asked Adam.

"I swear. But who do you think did? And how did they find out about my box? It's weird, isn't it?"

Lilith got up and went to the door. "It's perfectly obvious," she said. "You put them there yourself because you wanted to make up a mystery story and draw attention to yourself for a change."

Her words made me reel. Sometimes Lilith could say things that really stung. "Don't think I don't know that you get jealous sometimes," she continued. "I know you do . . ."

I opened my mouth to object, but it was true: I did get jealous sometimes and just as I knew what Lilith was feeling sometimes, of course it worked both ways and she knew what I felt, too. However, there was no way that I'd planted the gifts myself.

"Yeah, but . . . who wouldn't be jealous of you? You're always the best at everything, always first. But I swear on my grave and on the grave of our first cat, Monty, who is buried out there in the yard, I swear that I did not put those packages in there."

Lilith and Adam scrutinized my face.

"She's telling the truth," said Lilith.

"In that case, there has to be another explanation," said Adam. "I think, my leetle seester, that your hiding place was known to Mom or Dad. I think Mom felt sorry for you because you don't win prizes and that when she heard that Lilith won the poetry prize today she got you some presents to make up for it. Then she had them wrapped at the store, which is why they looked so professional."

Lilith and I nodded. It was exactly the sort of thing

that Mom would do. She was always going on about the importance of equality and sharing and looking out for those less fortunate than ourselves.

With Adam's possible explanation, I felt marginally better. I held my presents in my hands as we went up to bed. It was only when we had turned the lights off and Lilith and I had snuggled down in our beds that I remembered the computer printout, the banner announcing that I am a Zodiac Girl, and the gift tag saying, "For Eve Palumbo, this month's Zodiac Girl." Mom felt exactly the same as Dad and Adam when it came to horoscopes and astrology. She thought it was for fools. So it really couldn't have been her, after all. But if it wasn't her, who had left the packages? How had they known to hide them in my secret hiding place? Who the heck was P. J.? And what did he or she want with me?

Chapter Six

New House

"Matteo, *Matteo!* Put me down!" Mom cried as Dad gathered her up in his arms.

"But I'm going to carry you over the threshold," Dad said as he staggered up the pathway that led to the porch of our new house. "New house, new start."

Lilith glanced up and down the street behind where our car was parked. "How totally humiliating are our parents? I so hope that no one is watching and can see what a pair of lunatics we have for a mom and dad."

I laughed. I thought it was sweet and Lilith needn't have worried because the fiasco didn't last long. Even though Mom is slim, verging on skinny, Dad isn't as fit as he used to be and I could see that his knees were beginning to go. Seconds later, both of them fell in a heap on the front lawn.

"I really can't take any more of this," said Lilith, and she made a run for the front door and ducked inside. "We just got here and already I am so embarrassed!"

At that moment, I heard a phone ringing. Not mine

or Lilith's as we have Mozart's *Requiem* on ours. Adam downloaded it for us. He thinks it's a hoot and, to give him his due, no one else at our school has anything like it on theirs. No. This was a tone like someone was playing a church organ. It was weird.

"Where's that noise coming from?" asked Mom as she got up off the grass and brushed off her sweatpants.

Adam pointed at me. "You. It's coming from your backpack, Eve," he said.

"Aren't you going to answer it?" asked Mom.

I had an awful feeling that it was my new phone, so I shook my head. "I'll get it later."

"Come here," said Mom. "I'll answer it. It's probably one of your friends. I'll invite them over to help unpack." Before I could stop her, she'd grabbed my bag and next thing I knew she'd pulled out the phone from the side pocket where I'd put it. "What's this?" she asked. "This isn't your usual phone."

"I . . . I . . . it was a present."

Dad came to join her and looked at the phone which, although still ringing, had gotten quieter. "From who?" He took it from Mom, turned it over in his hand, and then gave it back to Mom. "It looks expensive. Who gave you this, Eve?"

I couldn't think of an answer fast enough and I felt myself going red. Mom's face clouded. "You haven't taken this from someone in a lower grade, have you?

I've read about the way teenagers mug each other for phones."

"Mom! How could you *think* that? Even for a second?" I asked. I felt appalled that she would think that.

Mom grinned. "Only joking, dear. No need to look so serious."

"Course we wouldn't think that," said Dad. "But maybe you bought it from someone who had mugged someone?"

"You have to be kidding! Don't you even know me? Your own daughter!"

Mom and Dad both laughed. "Only teasing you, Eve," said Dad. I gave them my best dirty look. They have a very strange sense of humor sometimes.

"But tell me where you did get it," said Dad. "It didn't just fall from the sky, did it?"

Adam snickered. "It might have. It was in her secret tin that was hidden behind the shed in the backyard at the old house."

"What secret tin?" asked Dad.

I shot Adam a dirty look, too, but he shrugged his shoulders as if to say, "What else could I say?" I shifted on my feet while I desperately scanned my mind for an explanation.

Mom looked from Adam to me, then back to Adam, then back to me. "I'm waiting," she said, "for the truth."

"It's from someone named P. J. I got it because I am this month's Zodiac Girl. And I found it in my secret tin when I went to dig it up last night."

"Secret tin?" asked Mom.

Dad sighed and looked wearily over at Mom. She looked like she was waiting for an explanation, but at that moment the moving van came down the street honking its horn. Dad started waving like mad at the driver to show him where to park.

Mom was still looking at me. "You and I are going to have a chat later, young lady," she said. Then she gave me back the phone and went off to join Dad in giving the movers their instructions.

"Aren't you going to answer it?" asked Adam.

I glanced down at the phone. It had started ringing even louder when Mom gave it back to me. "I suppose," I said, and I pressed the button that looked like it might be the answer button. "Hello."

"At last," said a foreign voice at the other end. "Is this Eve Palumbo who I am speaking vith?" I couldn't quite place the accent. He sounded like a mixture of Italian and Russian.

"Um . . . yeah. Who's this?"

"I am P. J. Vlasaova. I am phoning to say I am your guardian for one month."

"Excuse me?"

"You are da Zodiac Girl, *ja?*"

"Oh, that? Um. People keep telling me I am."

"You are da Scorpio, *ja, ja?*"

"*Ja, ja.* I mean, yes."

"Pluto is da ruling planet of Scorpio, so I vill be your guardian."

"Guardian? Ruling planet. But what does that mean?"

"It means you get da 'elp of me and da other planets for von month vile you are da Zodiac Girl. But from me especially as I am da ruler of da Scorpio."

"You and the *other* planets?" I asked as I made a face at Adam, who was listening in.

"*Ja.* Ve are all 'ere in 'uman form. Dis is no big secret unless you vant to make it von."

"Who is it?" Adam asked.

I put my hand over the phone. "Some guy named P. J. He sounds bonkers."

But Adam had stopped listening. He was watching a car come down the road. A chauffeur-driven black Mercedes with tinted windows.

"Vot is happening dere?" asked the voice at the end of the phone.

"My grandmother's just arrived. Er . . . I have to go. We're in the middle of moving," I said. I wanted to get him off the phone. Partly because I wasn't sure who he was and partly because I wanted to go and say hi to Nonna. Nonna is the Italian name for grandmother.

"*Ja, ja*, you go. Ve be meeting very shortly," said P. J. as Lilith came out of the house "Say hidie-hi to your grandmother."

"*Ja, ja*. Byeee," I said, and clicked the phone shut. I went to join Adam and Lilith who were waving at the car from the sidewalk.

Nonna's car slowed down and her driver parked in front of the moving van. Moments later, she stepped out in a haze of the signature perfume she always wore. It was called Zagara DiSicili and it smelled of orange blossom. I know because she gave Mom a bottle one Christmas. Mom never wears it, but I love to dab a little on for special occasions because it makes me feel grown up and rich.

Nonna looked elegant and stylish as always in a tailored suit and pumps. Her silver-gray hair lay sleek on her shoulders, where she had artfully thrown a red pashmina. She held out her arms to us. Nonna is the only person who Adam lets hug him. Lilith says it's because he's working on being her favorite grandson in the hope of inheriting a pile of her money. Nonna is loaded. She lives nearby most of the time, but her family is in the hotel business in Italy and owns a chain of six-star resorts on the Amalfi coast. Adam says that when she pops her Gucci clogs, she's going to leave one serious legacy. Not that I care. I just love her. She's one of the few people who can tell Lilith and me apart even when we're not standing side by side (a lot of people can see the difference when we're together, but not when we're apart), plus she knows everything about fashion and design.

"Bella bambinos," she said. "Eve, Lilith, still in black? I despair. Pretty girls like you should be wearing color, not be dressed like mourners at a funeral. And, Adam, so tall. Every time I see you, you've grown." She paused and looked at the house. "Hmm. So this is it, is it?"

We nodded, stood back, and looked at our new home with her. It was a white four-bedroom 19th-century house, set back from the road behind a small front lawn with shrubs and trees. It had two floors with large bay windows, a sweet porch at the front door, and a large backyard.

"What do you think, Nonna?" I asked.

She turned and gave me a conspiratorial wink. "I think it has potential. These old houses have good square rooms and high ceilings. I think it could be made very nice with a little input from the right people."

"Lilith and I are going to have our own rooms," I said.

"I heard," she said, and turned to look at me with her dark brown eyes that never missed a thing. "And how do you feel about that?"

Under her penetrating gaze, I felt myself blush and wondered if she could see how I really felt. "Okay, I guess. You know, new place, new chapter."

She looked up at the sky. It had clouded over since we arrived and looked like it might rain. She squeezed my arm. "That's the attitude. Now, let's go inside before it starts pouring down. I have a surprise early birthday present for you girls and a house-warming gift for you all." Then she giggled and winked at me again. "Not sure how your mom and dad are going to like it, but I think you will!"

Adam and I both linked our arms through hers and set off up the path.

"Hello, darlings," Nonna called to Mom and Dad, who glanced over from the back of the van and then exchanged worried glances. A visit from Nonna always involved some kind of interference as far as they were concerned. I couldn't wait. I loved it when she interfered.

When we got inside, we gave Nonna a quick tour of the ground floor and then went up to the bedrooms. Lilith's and mine were at the back of the house with the bathroom in between. Both were bare because the furniture hadn't been brought up yet, but they were light, airy rooms with wooden floors.

"Very nice," said Nonna with a nod of approval.

"I know. We have lots of plans," said Lilith. "I've been looking at goth sites on the Internet and have lots of ideas for both of us."

Nonna glanced over at me. "But I am sure Eve has

plenty of ideas of her own, don't you, angel?"

"I . . ." I started.

Lilith waved her hand as if dismissing me. "Yes, but we totally have the same taste."

"Is that right?" asked Nonna, and she glanced over at me again.

I looked at the floor. *Should I tell the truth?* I wondered. *Blurt out my secret?*

But Lilith was answering for me. "We always do stuff together, Nonna," said Lilith. "And even though we will have separate rooms, it will only be like one big room divided. Like we both have two bedrooms, if you know what I mean. I'll be in and out of hers, and no doubt she'll be in and out of mine."

I felt it wasn't the time for secrets so I steered Nonna back to the stairs and took her down to the kitchen. Outside, it was now pouring rain, so showing her the backyard wasn't an option. Even the movers seemed to have taken a break and were sheltering outside on the shed porch at the edge of the lawn.

"Sorry we can't offer you a drink yet, Mama," said Dad when he came in carrying a box. "Still unpacking, you know."

"Matteo, you need a haircut," said Nonna. Then she pulled a flask out of her bag and held it up. "No problem about the drinks. You know me: I always come prepared."

"In fact, it might be better if you came back at some other time," Dad continued. "We have an awful lot to do today and don't want you to feel neglected."

"Oh, I won't," said Nonna. "And, don't worry, I won't be in the way nor stay long. No. I came over to bring you a house-warming present."

Mom came in behind Dad. "You're too generous. You shouldn't have gone to the trouble," she said.

"Oh, I think I should have," she said. "I love to get you things. I thought long and hard about what to get you this time, and also for the girls for their birthdays on the twenty-sixth, and I think I've come up with the perfect solution. I know what you and my son are like when it comes to decorating—no time, always busy with your heads in your books and your jobs so . . ." She paused for effect and I could see that Mom and Dad were looking worried. "So, I've gotten you something to save you time and money."

Dad was still looking edgy. "Really, Mama, you shouldn't have. And—" he glanced outside at the rain that was lashing down as if it was trying to win the best rain competition—"we have to get going."

"Always so impatient! I won't take a sec," said Nonna, and she looked at her watch. "In fact, he'll be here any second."

"He? Who?" said Mom.

Nonna gave us all a big grin. "Your present. The

Transformer," she said.

Lilith looked like she was going to faint with delight. "Not *the* Transformer from the TV show?"

"What TV show?" asked Mom. Neither she nor Dad ever watched TV other than the odd documentary about history that bored the pants off Lilith and me.

"He's guest-hosting a TV makeover show," said Lilith.

"The very same," said Nonna. "We've used him for all the hotels in Italy and no one has an eye for decor like he does. Of course this was long before his time on TV."

Dad was looking completely perplexed. "Used him to do what in the hotels? What eye?"

"Interior design," Lilith replied. "He's the best."

"Best. But who is he exactly?" asked Dad. "Transformer sounds like an odd name to me. Like some sort of electrical appliance."

"The Transformer is only his name while he's doing this TV thing. His real name is P. J. Vlasaova."

And now it was my turn to feel faint, but not with joy, with surprise. "Did you say P. J.?" My question was drowned out by the loud ring of the front doorbell.

"That should be him now," said Nonna. "He likes to see the empty shell of a property before people fill it up with their bad taste, I mean furniture."

Dad's face had turned red and Mom looked like she was going to have a fit.

"So go and let him in," Nonna instructed. "I've

booked him for a month. He'll do whatever you want and I'll pay for it and at last the girls will have their fantasy bedrooms rather than living in some drab excuse for a room like in that last place."

Lilith and I raced to the front door. At the exact moment that we opened it, a flash of lightning lit up the porch and there he was: the Transformer. Tall, dark, wearing a black cloak, and looking every inch a goth prince as the sound of thunder rumbled overhead.

"Wow! Totally impressive," said Lilith.

The Transformer gave us a low bow. "P. J. Vlasaova at your service," he said.

Two seconds later, two other dark figures stepped out of the shadows and stood behind P. J. His strange-looking assistants, the blond with heavy black glasses and the stocky-looking man with the shaved head, looked more like bodyguards than interior designers.

"My assistants, Natalka and Oleksander," said P. J.

The two assistants bowed in exactly the same way that P. J. had moments earlier. I could hardly breathe. P. J. had the same voice and the same name as the man I'd talked to on the phone only a short time ago. He was also the same man I'd seen last night watching us in the cemetery. I was sure he was. Fear gripped my heart as he looked down at me and smiled.

Chapter Seven

Guardian

"*He's* P. J.," I whispered to Lilith as the Transformer went into the kitchen to be introduced to Mom and Dad while Natalka and Oleksander got busy in the hall with notepads and tape measures.

Lilith had gone all dreamy-eyed. "I can't believe he's here in our house. I can't wait to tell everyone at school after the break is over. Can you?"

"Ergh . . ." was all I could say. I felt frozen. Terrified, even. "But . . . he's the one I saw in the cemetery. I *swear*. And he's the one who left the phone. P. J. That was the name on the gift tag, *remember*?"

"Awesome," said Lilith. "Maybe I can ask him if I can have one as well."

"No. You can have mine, you really can. Please."

"Why? Don't you want it?"

"I . . . I . . ." I didn't want to tell her just yet that I was scared and then suddenly I had a brainwave. A way to get out of it and make everyone happy. I tugged her into the front room. "Listen, how about you pretend to be me and I pretend to be you? You can be the Zodiac Girl. I don't want to. It's not my thing and you love the Transformer more than I do."

I could see that Lilith was hooked. We'd swapped identities a million times when it suited us because most people had a hard time telling us apart. We had decided when we were little that it was one of the perks of being a twin. "You sure?"

I nodded. "Absolutely. We can do swapsies on something else later for me. Something you don't want. Okay?"

Lilith looked delighted. "Yeah. Cool."

Back in the kitchen, Nonna had introduced P. J. to Mom, Dad, and Adam, and I could see that although they were initially resistant they were slowly being won over. P. J. was clever and he appeared to be charming them by talking about decoration through the ages and what it said about each civilization. He was totally talking their language and it was like he was putting them under some kind of spell.

After half an hour, even Dad was talking about soft furnishings. I'd never seen anything like it! Dad doesn't do cushion covers. And then they trooped around after P. J. and his assistants like a bunch of crazed groupies and listened as he waxed lyrical about paints with names like Voltic Red and Urban Blue. And Dad and

Adam didn't snicker, not even once. Every now and then, P. J. glanced over at me, but I quickly looked away. He wasn't getting *me* under his hypnotic spell. One of us had to stay normal in case he turned my whole family into zombies and then came back to drink our blood.

When we got upstairs, Natalka and Oleksander continued measuring all the rooms and P. J., Lilith, and I went into Lilith's room. She told him of all her plans to make both her and my room into manifestations of goth fantasies. I noticed P. J. look my way a few times, but I looked out the window. *Don't make eye contact,* I told myself as we moved on to the other upstairs rooms. *Don't make eye contact.*

"Cat got your tongue?" asked Adam when we went back downstairs after we'd finished giving P. J. the tour and I hadn't said a word.

"No, the cat hasn't got my tongue because, in case you haven't noticed, we don't have a cat," I said, and I know that I sounded petulant and cranky and was probably going to get yelled at because Mom and Dad don't like us being like that. But I didn't. They both laughed as if I'd said something funny. It was really weird.

P. J. had a few words with his assistants and then sent them off to find materials. When they'd gone, he turned back to me. "Okay, I vant to look at your and

Lilith's rooms again," he said, "because I don't think I am quite clear on vot you *both* vant." He looked pointedly at me when he said "both."

Lilith had already set off down the hall and was looking back to see if we were following her.

"After you," said P. J.

"Thanks," I said, and trudged up the stairs. As soon as we got up to the rooms again, Lilith started off once more with her plans for the ultimate goth room and P. J. appeared to be going along with them. In fact, he had some good ideas of his own.

After awhile, he turned to me. "But you, Eve, vot do you vant?"

"I . . . I'm not . . . er, I . . ." I stammered.

P. J. turned to Lilith. "Lilith, dahlink," he said. "I'd love a glass of vater. Vould you please get me von?"

Lilith glanced at me and raised an eyebrow. "I'm Eve, not Lilith," she said.

"I'm Lilith," I said. Then I pointed at my sister. "Yes. She's Eve."

P. J. nodded. "Okay, den, *Eve*, pleasing you get me a glass of vater?"

I stared over at Lilith and telepathically sent her a message to say, *Please don't leave me alone with him.*

"You don't need to be afraid of being alone vith me," said P. J. as if he'd read my thoughts. "I don't bite," he said. Then he chuckled. "Only lying peoples I bite. But you are not lyings, are you?"

Lilith was about to leave the room so I had to think of something. "Um. No. Course not. Um. My sister got your nice phone and pendant, *didn't* you, Eve?"

Lilith nodded.

"And she's delighted to be a Zodiac Girl, *aren't* you, Eve?" I asked.

Lilith nodded again.

"Is she now?" asked P. J. "Okay. And she von't mind getting me vater to drink either den, vill she?" He flashed Lilith a smile and she set off immediately.

"Won't be a minute, Mr. Vlasaova," she said, and grinned back at him.

"Take as much time as you vish," said P. J.

As soon as she'd gone, he looked over at me. "So, Zodiac Girl, ven are you going to say vot you vant?"

"No. No. I'm Lilith. I told you. I'm not a Zodiac Girl."

P. J. raised an eyebrow. "You think dat I is being born yesterday? I don't think so."

"No, really. A lot of people get us mixed up. It's quite understandable."

"I am not getting you mixed up. You vere da second tvin born twenty minutes after da first tvin. You being Zodiac Girl. You are Eve."

I looked at the floor and wondered if I could keep up the charade. I glanced at him. He still had an eyebrow raised and by his expression I realized that it wasn't a good idea to keep up the hoax. He clearly wasn't falling for it.

"Okay, so I am Eve. But . . . I don't mind giving her the Zodiac Girl thing. Honest. We like to share everything."

"Dis is not possible, to 'and it over. And dis is a great honor. Many girls vould love to be da Zodiac Girl."

"I know. Lilith's one of them. She really admires you. I really don't mind letting her be a Zodiac Girl. As I said, I like to share."

"You are not sharing her likings for da room, I am thinking."

"What, the black walls? Well . . ."

"You are feeling frightened, Eve?" said P. J. in a soft voice.

"No. No. Course not. I don't get frightened."

"Eve. I am P. J. I am also Pluto."

I burst out laughing.

P. J. looked put out. "Vhy are you laughing? Vot do you know about Pluto?"

"It's a planet. And I know you can't be a planet. You mean that you come from Pluto? What am I saying? That's even weirder."

"I am saying dat I am Pluto."

"Then you're probably crazy," I said, and began to back away, "so I have every reason to be frightened."

"Is scaring you?"

"Duh? Was Dracula a vampire? Yeah, that scares me. I mean, you're saying being the Transformer is your day job, but that really you're Pluto. Excuse me, but I wasn't born yesterday either."

P. J. nodded. "I know dis. You vere born almost thirteen years ago on October da twenty-sixth. Okay. Dis is understandable. Is a lot to take in, but dere is no need to be frightened. I am not going to do anything spooky vooky. I am here to be helping. So, okay, let's be startings vith something not spooky vooky. Just think of me as P. J. Ve are changing da subject. No more crazy talk. Now. How about your room? How are you vonting it to look?"

I shrugged. "Lilith has already said, hasn't she?"

"She has said vot she vants but not vot you do. So, vot do you vant?"

I didn't dare say anything.

"Come on, let's go and look at your room," he said, and wandered out of Lilith's room and into mine. After a few moments, I followed him.

"Hmm," he said as he looked around. "Dis is a good room, *ja*?"

"*Ja*. I mean, yeah."

"And I am thinking dat seeing as you 'ave Taurus rising, and your sister, she has Aries, dat you are vanting different things?"

"Yeah."

"Taurus is ruled by da planet Venus and so is Libra. Did you know dis?"

"Not really."

"Planet Venus is da planet of love and beauty. People vith strong Taurus or Libra in der charts, they like da beautifuls things. Dey 'ave a great sense of beauty, so I am thinking dat you are not really vanting black valls in your room."

"I . . ." I didn't dare tell him how I really wanted my room. I hadn't admitted it to anyone.

"I saw da papers in your box, in da place vere I left your phone and charm. You are liking da phone, *ja*?"

"*Ja*. But . . . how did you know to leave them there?"

"I am P. J. Dis is vot I am saying to you, dat I am your guardian, *ja*? Von month as da Zodiac Girl, *ja*?"

"Yeah, but seems like you're going to be everyone's guardian for a month. Nonna's hired you."

P. J. laughed. "*Ja*, but dat is for doings da 'ouse. Dis is no problems. Dis is vhy I have assistants. Dey 'elp vith dat. *Ja*. But for you, is different. Ve have different things to do."

"Okay, then tell me how you knew where my secret tin was."

P. J. tapped the side of his nose. "I am P. J. and, okeee dokeee, 'ere comes more crazy stuff, but don't be scared, please. Dis is not scary vary. I *am* also Pluto and although dis is freaking you out at da moment, let me explain a little bit. As Pluto, I am da ruler of da Undervorld, ruler of all things hidden and secret, vich is vhy I know vot is in your 'eart, Eve Palumbo. I know your secrets and I know your fears. Together ve vill vork on dese fears. Make you stronger."

I had the strangest experience when he spoke, like he'd looked right inside me and had seen behind all my acts and masks to the true me. He was right. It was freaking me right out.

"Dis is okay. Now den . . ."

Lilith came charging back up the stairs with P. J.'s water. "Hey," she said. "I've had the *most* brilliant idea. You know how I can't make up my mind between the totally black walls or just the black ceiling? Well, we have two rooms, mine and Eve's . . . I mean, Lilith's, so how about this? We have one room as our bedroom and the other as, like, a day room for hanging out in and doing our homework and, that way, we can have different goth decors in each." She looked from me to P. J., very pleased with herself.

"He knows, Lilith," I said.

She gave me a dirty look and kicked my shin. "No. No. *I'm* Eve," she whispered.

I shook my head. "He *knows*."

Lilith looked embarrassed and stared accusingly at

me. "Did you tell him?"

"She did not need to tell me. I know secrets," said P. J. "I know many secrets dat people 'ave." For a few seconds, he stared at her and I swear she went red and looked at the floor. I'd never seen Lilith blush before and wondered, *Does she have secrets that I don't know about?* P. J. turned to me again. "So, Zodiac Girl, vot are you thinking of dis idea of your sisters? Sharing von room, living in da other?"

My mind went into a spin. *If we continued sharing, then I wouldn't be alone and so scared of the dark—that would be great. And maybe my nightmares would stop. But then I'd have to live with Lilith's style of room and that meant dark colors and weird posters of crows and dripping blood and I'd had enough of all that. And all that stuff is probably what's giving me the nightmares. I so wanted to do my room in my own way. In the way I'd been planning in my mind for weeks and weeks.*

"I—"

"How do you know secrets?" interrupted Lilith.

P. J. tapped the side of his nose. I decided it was time for her to realize that he was nuts even if Nonna *had* sent him.

"He says he's not just the Transformer," I said. "That's just his day job. Actually he is the planet Pluto. In fact, all the planets are here in physical form." I expected Lilith to laugh her head off when she heard this and then tell P. J. to get on his bike or asteroid or whatever planet he rode. But she didn't. Her face went through a spectrum of expressions: shock, disbelief, delight, then doubt, then puzzlement, then wonder.

"Awesome," she said.

P. J. smiled. "Thanks."

"Lilith, has someone boiled your brain?" I asked.

"Nobody boiled her brain. She has Aries rising. She is more impulsive den you. Spontaneous. Taurus rising makes you stubborn. I think vot I vill do is send over some of da other planet peoples. Some you liking more maybe. Let me think vot is in your chart. Is da encounter vith da Moon coming? Yes, dat vill 'elp. And Venus is vell aspected. I am 'aving a think, but more of us vill be coming your vay. *Ja, ja.*"

I felt my heart beat fast as fear flooded through me. More fears . . . that was the last thing I wanted.

Chapter Eight

First Night

Lilith stuck her head around my door.

"Night, Eve," she said.

"Night," I said.

"Exciting, isn't it?"

I nodded. "Yeah."

Lilith shut the door and I lay back and looked up at the ceiling in my new room. This was the moment I'd been dreading for weeks. The house felt quiet. The movers, Nonna, and P. J. had gone and all the activity in and out had stopped hours ago. We'd had a takeout pizza for supper and Mom and Dad unpacked as much as they could so we could settle in for the night. It was weird to be in this unfamiliar room with its smell of new paint and furniture polish. Mom and Dad had already been in to say goodnight before going to their room at the front of the house. Even Adam had been in to examine where I'd decided the bed should go (by the window on the right side of the room). It still looked a little bare, but at least Mom had gotten some curtains up and the bedding out and although most of my stuff was still in boxes, at least everything was in the right rooms, ready to be unpacked.

"Lights out now, Eve," I heard Mom call.

"In a few minutes," I called back. "Just doing something."

I heard her footsteps retreat and the sound of a door being closed. I took a deep breath and turned the light off. It was so dark. In our last room, the light from a lamppost on the street shone through the curtains, but because this room was at the back of the house overlooking the backyard , it was pitch black. I reached out and groped for the bedside light switch. I couldn't find it for a few seconds and felt myself tense as my imagination went into full throttle. *Someone's in the room and moved the light. I'm trapped. Any minute now, a hand is going to grab mine in the dark.* My mouth went dry, my chest felt tight, and my heart began to thud. *Confronting my fears? Tell me about it, P. J.*, I thought.

And then I found the switch, clicked it, and the room filled with light.

No one there.

Idiot. Of course there's no one here, I thought. But I couldn't bring myself to turn the light off again. *Best to make sure there really is no one here*, said a voice at the back of my mind. *Check in the closet and behind the curtains.*

I had to do it. It was like I was compelled, and no

way would I be able to settle if I didn't.

I got up, went over to the curtains, and looked behind them. Then I went over to the closet and looked inside. Next, I knelt down and looked under the bed.

No one there.

Obviously there isn't, idiot, I told myself. I got back into bed, turned off the light, and pulled the duvet cover over my head. If there was anyone there, if I couldn't see them, they couldn't see me. As I lay there, I was aware of the sound of my heart still thudding in my chest and my breathing. It sounded so loud. *I can't hear if anyone's there if I breathe so loud,* I thought, and I held my breath for a few seconds. I heard a dog bark outside, maybe on the next street. A car drove by. A stair creaked. I had to breathe out. *A stair creaked? A floorboard? Everyone's supposed to be in bed. Who's there? Who's on the stairs?* I heard the footsteps get louder, coming my way. The sound of the bathroom door opening and shutting next door. Phew. Probably Adam. Moments later, I heard the toilet flush. *At least there are people in the house. I'd hate to be here alone,* I thought as I turned over.

Now relax, Eve, I told myself. *Relax, count sheep. One, two . . .* I watched imaginary sheep jump over a fence. Some time later, I was still counting. *One hundred and ninety-nine, two hundred. Oh, it's no good. I can't sleep.* It was horrible lying there feeling that the whole world was happily sleeping away except for me in my strange room. I felt wide awake, with a knot in my stomach. There was no way I was going to sleep. *I may as well read a little,* I thought. I turned on the bedside lamp and looked at the boxes in the other corner of the room. I couldn't remember which ones my books were in.

I got up and found my backpack. My tin was in there and the zodiac phone was lying by the side of it. I had another look at it. It was very stylish. I turned it on and began to play with some of the buttons. It seemed easy enough to use. Maybe I'd take it in to show Mary at school. In fact, I could put her number in now. I could invite her over for a sleepover tomorrow. Yes, that would be great. If she came to stay, that would be one night at least when I wouldn't be all alone and scared. I went to the address section and was about to key in her number when I noticed that there were already ten numbers in there. *That's weird,* I thought as I scanned the list.

It read:

Joe Joeve: Jupiter
P. J.: Pluto
Hermie: Mercury
Dr. Cronus: Saturn
Sonny Olympus (Mr. O): Sun
Selene Luna: Moon

Captain John Dory: Neptune
Uri: Uranus
Nessa: Venus
Mario Ares: Mars

The other planets that P. J. mentioned, I thought. *But it's not possible that they are really planets. That's crazy. It must just be something to do with their names, like Eve means second woman and Lilith first woman. That's what it is. Hermie must mean Mercury, and so on.* On the main part of the screen, a tiny envelope showed that I had a text message. I pressed the READ button and the message came up.

This is the month when your hidden fears will rise to the surface. It is time to confront them. If in need, call any of these numbers. We are all here to help. We are all your friends.

Oh, are you? In that case, let's see if any of you can help me get to sleep, I thought. I scanned the list and decided against calling P. J. *Hmm. Dr. Cronus. Well, if anyone knows about not being able to sleep, a doctor should.* I pressed the button for Dr. Cronus.

A second later, a man's voice answered. "Who is this?" he asked. He sounded very cranky.

"Er . . . Eve Palumbo."

"Oh, you. The Zodiac Girl, if I'm not mistaken,

and probably another darned nuisance. You Zodiac Girls all are."

"But P. J. gave me this phone. He said you were all here to help and it had your number . . ."

"Do you know what time it is, young lady?"

"Eleven thirty."

"Exactly. I was fast asleep and I advise that you do the same."

"I *can't* sleep."

"No such word as can't."

"Well, I can't. As in cannot."

"So fresh. Have you tried counting sheep?"

"Yep. So far I got to two hundred."

"Ah. A classic case of insomnia. Okay, get back into bed and I am going to give you a lecture on the subject."

"A lecture?"

"You heard me."

"Dr. Cronus. Are you a real doctor?"

"I am."

"Of medicine and illness and stuff?"

"I am most certainly not! I am headmaster of a very exclusive private school. Now, have you gotten back into bed?"

There was something commanding in his tone and I did as I was told. "Yes."

"Then I'll begin. Insomnia is the perception or

complaint of inadequate or poor-quality sleep due to A) difficulty falling asleep, B) waking up frequently during the night with difficulty returning to sleep, C) waking up too early in the morning and/or unrefreshing sleep."

Boring, boring, I thought. He was also speaking in a monotonous voice and I felt myself growing drowsy as I listened.

"Millions are estimated to have occasional sleep problems, and about one in six have chronic insomnia. Insomnia can be described in terms of both duration and severity. Transient insomnia . . ."

On and on he droned, but I didn't dare interrupt him. I closed my eyes and lay back on the pillow.

". . . can be described as lasting from one night to a few weeks and is usually caused by events that alter your normal sleep pattern, such as traveling. Short-term insomnia lasts about two to three weeks and is usually attributed to emotional factors, such as worry, anxiety or stress. Eve, *Eve.* Are you there? You're being very quiet."

Zzzzzzzzzzzzzz.

Chapter Nine

A Visit

"I got you this as a special house-warming present," said Lilith the next day after we'd finished most of our unpacking and were having a snack break with Mary in my room. She handed me a roll of paper tied with a scarlet ribbon. "I got it from the poster store down by the market and I know you're going to love it. In fact, I almost didn't give it to you, it's so cool, but I wanted you to have something really special for when we moved in."

I untied the ribbon, unrolled the poster, and gasped. It was of a skeleton set against a huge red heart dripping blood and behind that a night sky threatening a storm. The skeleton was holding a scythe like the grim reaper. It was really menacing. I hated it.

"Wow. I . . . I don't know what to say," I stuttered.

"I know. It's so fabulously dramatic, isn't it?" asked Lilith.

"Er . . . you could say that," I said.

Mary glanced over my shoulder and burst out laughing. "Ye-uk. You two are so weird," she said.

"Wouldn't want *that* on my wall looking at me while I slept."

She amazed me. Simple. Honest. She just came out with it and didn't care what anyone thought. She'd come over to help with the unpacking and Lilith had filled her in on most of what had happened yesterday with P. J., but I was longing to get her alone so that I could give her my version, too.

"I suppose you'd like cute widdle kittens with bows around their necks, wouldn't you?" teased Lilith.

"Yeah, I would. Unlike you, who would probably like kittens with crow's heads or something strange," Mary returned.

I wish I could think up answers like that. I wish I didn't care so much that Adam and Lilith would be horrified if they saw what I'd really like on my wall.

Lilith reached into a bag that she'd brought into my room. "And look. Surprise! I went to the hardware store and bought us some paint samples." In a flash, she had unscrewed the tops off a couple and began daubing my wall with squares of what looked like black paint.

"This one is called Midnight Black," she said and then daubed another square. "And this one is Perfect Black. What do you think?"

Mary made a face. "They both look the same. Black," she said.

"Ah no," said Lilith. "There are subtle differences. You'll see when it dries. I've got some more in my room. I'll go get them." She put down the samples and went out the door.

Mary got up from the bed where she'd been sitting and picked up my zodiac phone from the window sill. "So, are you going to go along with her?" she asked.

"Dunno," I said. "I . . . sort of had some ideas of my own, but I think she'd be shocked."

"Lilith, shocked? I don't think so, not after having seen that skeleton poster. Surely your ideas can't be worse than that."

"Believe me, she will be totally freaked out when she sees what I have in mind."

Mary shrugged. "You're both nuts, but that's why I like you. And to each his own. I mean, as you know, I love a good scary movie, but personally I think macabre stuff sucks in a bedroom. Anyway, if it's your thing, then it's your thing." She turned the phone over in her hand. "This is a really tiny cell phone. Can you get me one?"

"No, no, and, Mary, sympathy, please. You heard Lilith tell you all about P. J. showing up and now she's taking over my new room. Help me. You're supposed to be my friend."

"Oh, just tell her to butt out and then do your own thing even if it will freak her out. She likes being freaked out. She wouldn't watch all those horror movies if she didn't. So, do you think you can get me a phone?"

I sighed. "I could try, but it doesn't work properly. Like, I tried to key in your number, but it wouldn't register and then I got a message from P. J. saying it was only for contacting him and his buddies."

"Awesome. I can't believe he's actually going to be here working. You are *so* lucky." Like Lilith, Mary had watched the TV house-makeover show and was a big Transformer fan.

"*Mary.* Have you even been listening to what's going on here?"

"Yeah. That the coolest thing in the world is happening to you because you are this month's Zodiac Girl. It was me that introduced you to the site, but you get to be the chosen one. I can't believe you tried to give it away, too. Like, where's your sense of adventure? What is the matter with you?"

I felt my heart sink. "I'm just not sure about any of it . . ."

"You need to chill, Eve. Relax and go with the flow," she said, like it was all that easy.

"But the flow would be to go along with Lilith's plan to have one bedroom and one living room."

"Yeah. Might be nice. But has something changed your mind? I thought you were looking forward to having your own room?"

"I was. I am," I replied. *If I could just get over my fear of the dark and my nightmares, I'd be fine.* Even though I'd finally fallen asleep last night, I'd still had bad dreams about faces appearing at the window and figures in hoods lurking in shadows. "I . . . P. J.'s coming back tomorrow with his assistants and I said I'd let him know what I want by then." I was torn between wanting Lilith's company because I was scared and wanting to have my own space for the first time in my life.

"Hey, Mary," Lilith called from her room. "Come and listen to this."

Mary got up. "Catch you later," she said.

I nodded and five minutes later I could hear loud music coming out of Lilith's room. *At least she's forgotten about showing me more black paint samples for the time being,* I thought as I gazed out the window and up at the sky. The rain had cleared and the Sun was struggling to come through. As I stared up at the clouds, I noticed a white bird. *It's a dove,* I thought as it flew toward our house. And toward the trees in the front yard. In fact . . . it was coming right at me! *Oh god,* I thought. *I hope it's not going to fly into the window.* I've seen birds do that before when the sun is at a particular angle. But no, the dove stopped just short of the window and hopped onto the windowsill. It pecked on the glass with its beak and looked right at me. It had something fastened to its leg.

I opened the window and the bird hopped closer, all the while looking at me. Around its leg was a tiny roll of paper. I unfastened it and the bird flew off.

I shut the window and unrolled the paper.

Venus is well aspected in your chart this week bringing harmony and peace to a troubled situation.

In the hallway, I heard the phone ring and then minutes later, Mom appeared at my door. "That was P. J., dear."

"Oh. Did he want to talk to me?"

Mom shook her head. "No. He asked that I drop you off at the Pentangle Beauty Salon in Osbury and said that someone there is going to show you some ideas for your room. And he said to take your tin. What tin? Does that make sense to you? Is that the one you hid before we moved?"

"Um, yeah. It's just a box with some . . . er, stuff in it. But someone? Who?"

"Someone named Nessa. I need to go into the village, too, so get your things and we'll be off."

"Should I tell Lilith? Oh, and Mary's here."

Mom shook her head. "We won't be long. P. J. said to bring just you because Lilith already has her ideas clear in her head. P. J. seemed concerned that you were maybe just going along with your sister. Is that true, sweetheart?"

"I . . . I'm not sure what I want yet."

"Then let's go! Let's go and see what this lady has to show you."

I hesitated for a moment and then blurted out, "Mom, I'm not sure about this P. J. guy."

Mom gave me a mysterious smile and beckoned me out of my room. "Neither was I at first so I Googled him as soon as your dad set up the computer this morning. Come with me." She led me downstairs to the back room where the computer was. "Take a look at this." She typed "The Transformer" into Google and then clicked the mouse. A page came up showing a whole list of links. She clicked on the first one. "I'll leave you to read while I go get ready."

It was amazing. Page after page of makeovers that he'd done. Houses he'd transformed. Different styles, different tastes—it seemed like there was nothing he couldn't do and I had to admit that in each and every one he'd made a stunning transformation.

Mom came back in after awhile and stood behind my shoulder. "At first I thought Nonna had some nerve hiring this stranger, but actually she couldn't have picked a more perfect present and it's very generous of her. As his site says, P. J.'s the name, transformation's the game."

"You don't . . . find him a bit spooky?"

"Oh, you mean his Victorian poet look? Not really. I think it makes him look rather romantic," she said as she gazed dreamily at P. J.'s picture on the screen.

"Mom! You've got a crush on him!"

Mom giggled and put her index finger to her lips. "Shh," she said. "Don't tell your dad. But, really, P. J. can work wonders here and it means your dad and I can relax and not worry about it. It's a bit of a relief, to be honest. I don't know the first thing about decor or style, but I do know what looks good when someone else does it. So, come on, let's go see what this mystery person has to show you."

We arrived in Osbury about fifteen minutes later and looked for a beauty salon called Pentangle.

"Over there," I said as I spotted the name above a white shop window. We went over and tried to peer inside, but it was hard to see because there was a white venetian blind up.

"Let's ring the bell," I said, and pressed the silver buzzer I could see next to the door.

Just as the door opened, the sun came out of the clouds, illuminating the figure standing in front of us. The sight couldn't have been more of a contrast with the dark figure of P. J., who had stood on our porch in the storm only yesterday. For one thing, this person was female, dressed in white jeans and a tight top. She was a blond babe. *Adam would go mental if he saw her*, I thought as I said "hi." She was a living, breathing Barbie.

She beamed a wide smile, showing perfect white teeth. "Can I help y'all?" she asked in a Southern accent.

"Yes," said Mom. "P. J. sent us. You must be Nessa, right?"

"Yeah. I've been expecting you. Come on in."

"Well, actually, I was hoping to leave Eve here with you while I go get some supplies from the supermarket."

"Of course, doll. P. J. told me that you all just moved yesterday."

I had to hold myself back from laughing. No one had ever called my mom anything like that before. Professor, yes. Doll, no. She didn't seem to mind, though, and she nodded.

"Yes, it's madness."

"I can imagine. Eve and I will be just fine here."

"I'll be back in about an hour, then, okay?"

"Take your time, hon," said Nessa. "We'll find plenty to talk about, right, Eve?"

"Um, yeah."

Mom set off in the direction of the supermarket and Nessa ushered me inside. "Well, Zodiac Girl, where should we start?"

I hesitated for a second and wondered whether to try to pretend that I was Lilith and that Eve couldn't make it, but she saw me pause. She chuckled and then nudged me playfully. "And don't you try any of that twin swappin' malarkey. P. J. told me you might. Bet you and your sis have quite a giggle sometimes."

"Sometimes," I admitted. I liked her. She exuded warmth and seemed like fun, but not Adam and Lilith's spook-everyone-out kind of fun. "Yeah, we have. About this Zodiac Girl thing . . ."

"So, what do you think of my place, darlin'?" Nessa asked, changing the subject.

I looked around at the decor as I set down my backpack with my tin in it. It was lovely. Simple but stylish. The walls and ceiling were white and it had the mirrors that you'd expect in a salon, but painted in between the mirrors were entwined silver leaves and along the top of the walls were patterned borders of silver.

"Those are Celtic patterns," said Nessa as she saw me look up. "I've just had it done. I like to change it once or twice a year."

"Once or twice a year?"

"Yeah. I like so many different colors and looks, why keep it one way forever? I think people get stuck in one style and it all gets stagnant, you know? I had this place decorated like a fairyland last year, with little twinkly lights everywhere. It was lovely. I'm not usually part of P. J.'s decoratin' team, though. Most of the time I run the beauty salon here and occasionally I teach night classes in how to find your inner goddess."

"But you're going to show me some ideas for

interior design, aren't you?"

"Yes, but all in good time. First make yourself comfy. I thought we could relax a bit." She glanced down at my bitten fingernails then quickly looked away as if she didn't want to draw attention to them. "How about a pedicure and some girl time?" she suggested.

It wasn't what I expected, but ten minutes later I was lying back on a reclining chair while a blond girl named Chantelle massaged my feet with perfumed oil. Gentle music played in the background. I'd never had a pedicure before and it felt fabulous.

"Smells gorgeous," I said to Nessa who was in the chair next to mine having her feet done by a girl named Sennah.

"Yeah. It's a mix of frankincense and jasmine. Lovely. Reminds me of home."

I nodded. "I like the music, too."

"Yeah. Uri from the cyber café down the road put it together. It's a sort of chill-out CD. He did it on the computer."

"Cool," I said, and settled back, closing my eyes. As Chantelle worked her magic on my feet, I began to feel myself relax and a warm, cozy feeling began to spread through my body. Before I knew it, I had drifted off. Nessa must have let me sleep because when I awoke it was half an hour later, the pedicure girls had gone, and Nessa had brought me a hot drink.

"Tea, lemon, and a few secret ingredients," she said as she placed the mug beside me. "How are you feelin', darlin'?"

"I think I've died and gone to heaven," I said. "I feel all floaty and light. It's lovely here."

Nessa smiled. "We try to make people feel good. And it's important to have balance in your life. Work, play, relaxation, all in the right amounts."

"I agree," I said, and made a mental note to make pedicures a part of my life from then on.

"Now then, doll. P. J. thought you might like to hear some of my ideas for decoratin'."

"Yes, I'd love to."

"But, the thing is, I'm me. And you might not like what I like. So, before I show you, what I want to know is how you see your room yourself. Got any ideas?"

I hesitated again. I'd never told anyone how I saw it, not Lilith, not even Mary, but Nessa looked like she might understand and maybe even like my ideas, and I was feeling so warm and fuzzy and safe that I felt like I could tell her anything.

"My sister, Lilith, is really into goth and she wants to do her room, maybe both our rooms, in that style, you know, dark, spooky posters on the wall—"

"But that's your sister's vision, not yours," Nessa said gently. "I can see already that wouldn't be your style. You want something different, don't you?"

I nodded. "I think so, but I think people who know me, know us, might be shocked."

"So, do it the way you want and maybe next year, like me, you'll change your mind. That's okay. A coat of paint doesn't cost much. A few posters. A few accessories. Get a few magazines, have a flick through, that's what I do. I keep all the pages with interiors I like in a special file."

"So do I! I . . . I . . ." I knew that I didn't need to see her magazines. I already knew what I wanted because I had been collecting my ideas for months now in my secret tin. "But I . . . I have a problem, Nessa."

"Most Zodiac Girls do," she said. "Often that's why they're Zodiac Girls—they're at a turnin' point in their lives or have come up against some obstacle. You've just moved, haven't you? That's pretty major."

"So why isn't my twin sister a Zodiac Girl, then?"

"She's probably more comfortable with what's happenin'. Is that right?"

I nodded.

"So what's this problem of yours? You don't have to tell me if you don't want to."

"I . . . I've never told anyone."

"Your secret's safe with me. Promise. Cross my heart."

"And promise you won't laugh?"

"Not unless it's really funny," she replied with a smile. She gave my arm a gentle squeeze. "If something's botherin' you, it's best to get it out. A problem shared is a problem halved. If you keep it all bottled up inside, it can feed on itself and grow and grow until it becomes like a monster inside of you."

"That's *exactly* what it's like," I said.

"Come on, then. Let it out."

"Okay. My . . . my problem is that . . . and I know it sounds silly and childish, but I . . . am scared of the dark."

"I don't think that's silly. Lots of people are scared of the dark."

"Not in my family," I said, and I quickly filled her in on Adam and Lilith's spook nights.

She listened patiently and I could tell by her eyes that she was sympathetic. "Why do you think you can't tell anyone?"

"Already I am second best at everything. Lilith is the perfect twin. She gets all the prizes. She's smart and fearless and writes amazing poetry and I tag along behind her never able to catch up. If she and everyone else knew that I was a big sissy and scared of the dark on top of being such a total loser, it would be *so* humiliating. *That's* why I can't tell anyone."

"Oh, you poor doll," said Nessa.

I nodded. "And that's my problem, see? I can't decide. If I share a room with Lilith, then I won't be scared at night because she'll be there—I feel just about okay if someone's there with me—but if I do share with her I won't have my own room, which I was so looking forward to decorating myself."

"And what in your heart would you really, really like to happen?"

"Not to be scared anymore."

Nessa nodded. "If you can get over that, you'll be free. You'll be able to go anywhere and not be frightened. Feel like sharing the plans you have for your room?"

I went over to my backpack and pulled out my secret tin. I turned and held it over my chest. "I, er . . . I've been collecting some ideas in here for how I'd like it to look."

Nessa beckoned me to bring her the tin.

"I . . . but I've never shown anyone these. Promise you won't be shocked."

Nessa winked. "I'll do my best."

I decided that I could trust her. "Okay, but it's a secret."

"Okay," she said.

I flicked through and removed my private poetry (I wasn't ready to show anyone that yet!) and handed over the rest of the papers from the box. She glanced through them and nodded, looked up, and smiled. "This is much more you." Suddenly she laughed. "But it won't be much of a secret if you fix your room up like this."

She spread the papers that I'd cut out from magazines on the floor. Each and every one of them was gorgeously, gloriously . . . pink.

Chapter Ten

Makeover Magic

"Be brave," said Nessa after I'd expressed my fear of revealing my plans to my family, and that was exactly what I intended to be. I left her salon feeling relaxed and encouraged—plus I had bright pink toenails to match my fantasy room decor.

I told Mom my plan to go pink on the way home. She didn't bat an eyelash. "Whatever you like, dear," she said. "You have to live with it."

And so my first secret is out to one member of my family. One down, I thought as I got out of the car when we reached home, but then I should have known that Mom would be easy. She just wasn't interested in that sort of thing. I went to Lilith's room. She and Mary were on the floor painting each other's toenails. Pearly white for Mary; vampire red for Lilith. I wasn't surprised to see that Lilith was doing her toenails, too. We often end up doing the same things when we're apart. It's a twin thing.

"I have something to show you," I said, and before

I lost my nerve I pulled out my pink plans and laid them on the floor.

"*This* is how I want to do my room," I blurted.

Mary and Lilith glanced over the papers. Mary looked up at me and gave me the thumbs up. Lilith looked confused.

"You are joking," she said.

"Um . . . no. It's how I'd like my room, so, you see, we can't share because we have such different ideas."

Lilith stared up at me, trying to figure out whether I was kidding. "Ohmigod. You're serious," she announced after a few seconds.

I nodded. "And . . . and don't try to talk me out of it because it's what I really, really want." And I left the room before she could say a word.

I went to bed that night feeling concerned about Lilith's reaction. *Relax,* I told myself. *One step at a time. I was brave and told Lilith my plans—that's a start.* At least I didn't have to worry about the dark because Mary was staying over and, when I finally got to sleep, I slept well. I felt that my life had maybe begun to turn a corner.

P. J., his assistants, and a team of decorators arrived first thing the next day, and it was like watching a makeover program on fast forward. They started on the ground floor and everywhere there was noise, dust, knocking, and nailing. At one point, when the decorators were having a coffee break, I cornered P. J., who was supervising everything, and showed him my plans. He seemed to like them. He was as encouraging as Nessa had been and I began to think that maybe he wasn't as spooky as I'd first imagined. He even threw in a few ideas of his own that I liked.

"Dis is more you," he said as he glanced over the room plans again. "It's good you are telling people vot you vant in your room, but Nessa said dat dere is more dat you need to say, *ja*?"

"Everything I told her was a secret!" I said.

"Vot did I tell you before? I am knowing all secrets because I am Pluto, planet to do vith all things hidden. Dis is my special talent, if you like. I can't help knowing dese things."

I knew he was referring to my fear of the dark. "Well, don't tell the others, okay?"

He crossed his heart. "I vould never do dat. Dis is up to you ven you are ready, and I am thinking dat you vill be ready soon, and dis is vhy you are da Zodiac Girl."

"Because I'm afraid of the dark?"

"Because you are ready to be facing dis fear and I and my fellow planeties are here to help."

"But how?"

P. J. looked thoughtful for a moment. "Da next thing coming in your chart is conjunction between da Moon and Mercury."

"Mercury's the planet of communication, isn't it?" I asked. I'd read in my *City Girl* magazine in our weekly horoscope that there was something to do with Mercury's influence this week.

P. J. nodded.

"So what does that mean exactly?"

"It vill mean vot you make of it," P. J. replied. "How you respond. Like da Sun shines on all of us but some people choose to be out and sunbathe, others stay indoors or put a hat on. Understand?"

"Sort of. But . . . will some of the stuff that's happening to me apply to Lilith even if we don't have the same rising signs?" I asked.

"Yes. You are right. Some if it is very particular to you, Zodiac Girl, while other things happen to all Scorpios. Even so it is always up to da individual vot dey make of it. Dis veek is the time for opening up and communicating for all Scorpios, but for you, you vill be getting special help. Understand?"

"Sort of," I said.

He's talking in riddles, I thought, but later that night, just after we'd gotten ready for bed, Lilith came into my room.

"Hi," she said, and she shifted about on her feet as if she was feeling a little awkward.

"Hi," I replied.

"I . . . I have something I need to say. I . . . I just

wanted to say that I am sorry if I have been a bossy boots and didn't really consult you about our rooms. I guess I can be a little bossy and, in the future, please just tell me if I am going on about anything, and what you really want."

"Okay," I said. "I . . ." *Tell her now! Tell her now that you're scared of the dark and are dreading being by yourself,* said a voice in my head. "I . . . I . . ." I couldn't bring myself to say the words.

"I what?" asked Lilith.

"I think your room will be fab," I said. "It's just not what I want at the moment."

"I can't wait for our first sleepover in there. We can tell ghost stories and everything. It will be great."

I nodded. I didn't want to miss out on that. Right.

She gave me a hug goodnight and then I was alone in my new bedroom once more. I heard Mom call "Lights out," and I knew that I had to face my fears.

I turned the light out and the room disappeared into darkness. I squeezed my eyes shut, but it was dark in there, too. My mouth went dry and my heart began to pound, *boom, boom, boom,* like a big drum. I put my hand up to my mouth and nibbled on my nails. I thought about calling Dr. Cronus so he could bore me to sleep again, but he'd sounded so annoyed last time that I didn't dare. Maybe I should call Hermie, since he's the one for communication, seeing as there's some aspect to him or something. *Maybe that's what P. J. was trying to tell me,* I thought. I switched my light back on, found the phone and pressed the button for Hermie.

I got his voicemail. "Hi, ZG. See you in the morning," said a man's voice.

Wow! How did he know I was going to call? Not even I knew that. And, anyway, I need you now, I thought as I got back into bed. I lay down, trying to make myself relax, but as on the first night I had spent in my room alone I got a strong compulsion to check everywhere to make sure there was nothing and nobody in the room. *And you have to do it ten times,* said a voice in my head. I got up and looked behind the curtains ten times, under the bed ten times and in the closet ten times.

I got back into bed and turned off the lights. My heart was still beating loudly in my chest and there was a knot of tension in the pit of my stomach. No *way* was I going to be able to sleep feeling like this.

Call Nessa—she'll understand, I thought, and I got out of bed and dialed Nessa's number. That was also on voicemail. "*Hi, ZG, think happy thoughts,*" she said.

I got back into bed. *Think happy thoughts, think happy thoughts.*

I made myself think of all my favorite things. *Peach melba with raspberry sauce. Vanilla ice cream with hot fudge. Swimming in the sea in Italy on vacation. Laughing with Lilith when we swapped identities and got away with it. Mary trying to tell a joke and forgetting the punch line.* Yes, it seemed to be working. *Yes, thinking happy thoughts. I can do this.* And then I heard a noise at the window and froze. *Was there somebody there? Should I look? Yes. Noooooo. What if there was someone there and it was a face looking back at me? Happy thoughts, happy thoughts.* I pulled the covers over my head. *I hate this,* I thought, *but I have to get over it. I have to. Count sheep, one two three. Oh god, the sheep are turning into little monsters. Even their wool is turning dark and horns are growing out of their heads and they're coming at me. Go away. Nice sheep come back. Little lambs. Think little cute fluffy lambs. Oh! What was that? Another noise. Someone's out there. A floorboard creaking. Has someone come into my room? I'm afraid to look.* And then I almost leaped out of my skin as my zodiac phone rang. I switched on the light and went to the phone.

"Hello, darlin'," said Nessa's voice. "Sorry I couldn't get to the phone earlier. Can't sleep?"

"No. It's awful. I'm so tired, but I feel like someone put a belt around my waist and pulled it tight . . ."

"Slow down, darlin'," said Nessa. "Now, have you tried thinkin' happy thoughts?"

"Yep. Tried that. But I kept thinking about faces at the window and people creeping up on me—"

"No, no, that won't do. Now, get into bed. Lie back and do as I say," said Nessa.

I did as I was told. Just hearing her voice made me

feel better. "Okay, now I want you to take a deep breath, right into your stomach. You doin' that? Like your tummy's a beach ball and it's blowin' up big as you breathe in and deflatin' as you breathe out. And say to yourself, my breathin' is calm and regular."

"Yes," I replied as I inhaled and exhaled. "My breathing is calm and regular."

"Now, focus on your toes, okay? I want you to tighten your toes. Tighten, tighten. Now let them go. Good. Now focus on your feet. Tighten them up. Okay? Now let them go and think, my feet are heavy."

I tightened and relaxed as Nessa slowly went up the whole body—calf muscles, knees, thighs, stomach, chest, hands, arms, neck—and I felt each part relax and grow heavy as she directed.

"Now tighten up the muscles of your face, tighten your jaw. Now let your jaw drop as you relax it."

I didn't hear her after that as I was fast asleep. Once again, phone-a-planet had sent me off to sleep. ZZZZZZzzzzzzzzzzzzz.

Chapter Eleven

Motorcycle Messenger Boy

"What the devil!" said Dad, and he ran to the front window on Friday morning, the last day of our school vacation.

Lilith put down her breakfast toast and dashed to join him. I wasn't so fast. Couldn't be bothered, in fact. I was too tired to dash anywhere as I'd hardly slept all week. It hadn't gotten any easier after Nessa's call because, before I knew it, another night had come around. And another. And each time the same old fears came up, no matter how many times I told myself to relax. I'd been awake into the early hours while I did battle with my imagination and fear of the dark before finally falling asleep due to exhaustion.

"Come on, Eve," said Lilith. "You have to see this."

I dragged myself to my feet and joined her and Dad at the window. There was the strangest sight: A motorcycle had stopped in front of our house and on the back, dressed head to foot in black leather with her arms wrapped around the man in front, was Nonna. She saw us gaping at her and gave us a cheery wave.

Dad tutted. "Whatever will that crazy woman get up to next!" he said.

"Way to go, Nonna," said Lilith as the man on the front of the bike took off his helmet to reveal that he was a handsome boy, about nineteen or twenty years old maybe, with shoulder-length glossy brown hair, which he shook loose. "She's got herself a boy toy!"

Nonna got off the bike and headed up the path while Dad went to let her in, huffing and puffing with disapproval as he did so.

"Do you really think that you should be cavorting around like a *teenager* at your age?" asked Dad.

Nonna laughed. "I think that's *exactly* what I should be doing," she replied, then looked at us. "Now, you girls, I have my instructions. P. J. said that since your mom and dad will be at work later today I have to get you out of the decorators' way. It can't be much fun listening to their racket. So, Lilith dear, you and I are going shopping."

Lilith looked pleased. Shopping with Nonna was always great fun because she loved to spoil us and buy us presents.

"Can I come?" I asked, although I knew I already had a prior appointment, the one that I had been dreading for weeks, with the counselor to talk about my nail biting.

"We wouldn't forget you, my angel," said Nonna. "No. You're going with Hermie, outside."

Ah. Hermie—that's the name for Mercury, the winged messenger, I thought, as I glanced out at him again. He saw me looking and waved.

"What? On the bike?" Dad, Lilith, and I chorused, but Dad said it with surprise, Lilith said it with envy, and I said it with anticipation. I've always wanted to ride a motorcycle.

"Absolutely, Matteo," said Nonna. "Don't worry, I've checked him out. No way I'd let a granddaughter of mine go off with a complete stranger. I know Hermie's grandfather, Dr. Cronus. We play bridge together in Osbury. He's the headmaster of a very exclusive private school, you know."

"Well, only if Eve wants to go on that thing," said Dad. "And where's he going to take her? I don't like this at all."

I peeked out again at Hermie. He looked friendly and, as Lilith had said, he was a total babe. Maybe we could have a picture taken together and I could show it around school. Everyone would be so envious.

"Oh, for heaven's sake, Matteo, I'm your mother. Have a little more trust. Hermie is here to take Eve to see her counselor today. No doubt you'd forgotten."

Dad looked embarrassed for a moment. "Marissa

asked me to organize a ride for Eve because you and she will be at work," said Nonna.

"Yes, but we didn't expect a motorcycle," said Mom coming in behind us with a pot of coffee. "I thought you might give her a ride in your car."

"And good morning to you, too, Marissa," said Nonna. "Honestly, the thanks I get from this family. I don't know why I bother."

I put my arms around her waist. "I'd love to go on the bike," I said.

"So would I," I heard Lilith mutter behind me. She looked really jealous.

Fifteen minutes later, I was wearing a helmet and clinging on to Hermie's jacket as we roared along the streets. It was a lovely, clear autumn day, not a cloud in the sky, and I felt my spirits rise as people on the sidewalk stopped and stared at us whizzing by. We rode through Osbury, past the shops, past Pentangle Beauty, Salon and along a country lane.

"Not much farther," Hermie called back. "You okay back there?"

"Yep," I replied.

We passed a church, went up a hill past a public garden that advertised it had a sacred well and was a sacred site, and just after that Hermie stopped his bike. I climbed off and looked around.

"Wow, pretty," I said. To my right, over a small stone wall, there was a panoramic view of fields stretching as far as the eye could see. To our left there was a soft hill with a tower up at the top.

Hermie pointed to the hill. "Up there," he said.

"There must be some mistake," I said. "I have an appointment to meet my counselor. Call Nonna or Mom. I think you've got the wrong place."

"Nope, this is it," said Hermie, and he set off up the hill. "She said to meet her at the top. She often likes to work out in the open."

I followed him up the graduated steps that became steeper and steeper the higher we got. I had to stop every now and then to catch my breath because it was farther up than it had looked from down below. The view got better the higher we climbed. It was like being on top of the world in the very center, and we could see for miles and miles in every direction. Hermie didn't seem bothered by the ascent at all. He strode on up as if we were walking on level ground.

As we got closer to the top, I could see the tower more clearly. It was a tall structure with open arches in front and back. Just outside, I could make out a figure. A lady with long white hair to her waist who was dressed in an ankle-length, pale aquamarine dress. She looked like a lady from the time of King Arthur and Camelot.

Hermie beckoned me on and then waved to the

woman, who waved back. She was beautiful, like a fairy queen, with clear, white skin and green-blue eyes that matched her dress. Around her throat she wore a pendant of a crescent Moon.

"Zodiac Girl," she said when we caught up to her.

"Uff, uff, yes," I said as I struggled to catch my breath.

"I'm Selene Luna," she said. "Your mom booked an appointment with me."

I stared up at her in awe. "Yes, but . . . are you *really* the counselor?"

She nodded and indicated a grassy knoll on which to sit. I sat down and she joined me.

"It is lovely up here, isn't it?" she asked.

I nodded.

"I like to work out in the open when I can," she continued as Hermie flung himself down on his back, put his hands behind his head, and stared up at the sky. "I mean, why be indoors where it's stuffy when you can be out in the fresh air?"

"Um, yeah." Inside I was wondering what on earth we were going to do. I knew a few girls who had gone for counseling and, by all reports, it had been nothing like this.

"So. I'm told that you have a fear of the dark?" she asked.

I nodded although it seemed ridiculous. My fears last night seemed a million miles away from the light, open place we were in and the two beautiful people who were next to me.

"And no one in your family knows?" asked Hermie.

Hmph, I thought. *That Nessa has a big mouth. Is there anyone who doesn't know my secrets?*

"Fear not," said Selene, as if picking up on my thoughts. "Only the ten planets know about your fear. We have to or else we could not help and that is our role for you during your special month."

"Yeah. Um. About that planet people thing. Correct me if I'm wrong: you're all part of a family that likes to pick names of planets?"

Hermie and Selene exchanged glances as if they found what I'd said funny. Then Selene nodded.

"You could put it like that. Our names are derived from the planets, but each Zodiac Girl interprets our presence in a different way," she said.

"We'll leave it to you to decide who or what we are," said Hermie. "It doesn't really matter. What matters is what you make of this month. Let me ask you something: can you explain who you really are aside from your name and your physical description?"

When he put it like that, I realized that I couldn't. I, Eve Palumbo, was as big a mystery to myself as the planet people were. "Guess not," I replied.

"Are you ready for the session to begin?" asked Selene.

"I suppose," I said. "What should I do? Do I need to talk?"

"You can do whatever you like. Normally I run these sessions by myself because some people like to keep their counseling sessions private—but for you it's different. The Moon and Mercury are conjunct in your chart at the moment. Mercury governs communications, among other things, and the Moon governs emotions and . . . oh, I'll make it easy. Today is a good day for communicating your feelings if you'd like to. So, first question, do you mind Hermie staying and chipping in now and then? He really is a whiz at all things to do with communication and might be of some help."

Hermie flashed me an irresistible smile.

"No. He can stay," I said. I smiled back at him.

"Good," said Selene. "How are you feeling, Eve?"

"Fine," I said. I did feel fine, but then I began to feel nervous because I could see that Selene was looking at my nails or rather lack of them.

"But you don't always."

"Guess not."

"Fine is *F. I. N. E.*," said Hermie. "*F* for freaked out, *I* for insecure, *N* for neurotic, and *E* for exhausted. Sometimes people just blurt out, "Oh, fine," but if you dig a bit deeper you discover that they're *F*reaked out, *I*nsecure, *N*eurotic and *E*xhausted."

"Hey, I'm not *that* bad," I said. "I mean I'm okay when I say fine."

"Okay, fine," said Hermie, and I wasn't sure if he

was teasing me or not.

"How do you feel when you, say, bite your nails?" asked Selene.

"I get nervous sometimes," I replied.

"Tell me about how that feels," said Selene. "Try to remember the last time you felt like that. You can close your eyes if that helps."

I closed my eyes and made myself remember how I'd felt the night before. "Okay. Sometimes it's as if there's something inside of me, something horrible, like a poisonous snake all tight and curled up in the pit of my stomach that makes me feel my worst. I feel as if every part of me is as tense as it possibly could be and I've gotten locked like that and don't have the key to undo it. And being this way makes me imagine things, makes me scared."

Selene nodded as I opened my eyes. "Fear. It can paralyze you."

"But sometimes fear can be good," I said, "like if you're in a situation and your senses tell you that you're not safe—like when you're walking down a road and you get a feeling that something or somebody's not right. Sometimes your fear can be your friend because it can warn you about something."

"But more often than not," said Selene, "what we fear is in our imaginations and can build and build and ruin our lives."

"Fear is *F. E. A. R.*," said Hermie. "*F* for false, *E* for expectations, *A* for appearing, *R* for real. *F*alse *E*xpectations *A*ppearing *R*eal. As Selene said, we get scared of something we've imagined; it's not even real. It can't be dismissed because it can make you feel awful. The *feeling* of fear is all too real."

"That's the fear we're going to talk about today," said Selene, "because at those times, the best thing you can do is reach out and tell someone. Tell your mom or your sister or your friend."

"No! I can't do that. Can't. Can't. *Can't*," I insisted.

"Why not?" asked Hermie.

"Mom and Dad would think I was pathetic. They don't do feelings; they only do reason and logic. I'd have to explain *why* I feel like that sometimes, and I couldn't begin to. Adam and Lilith would think I was a sissy and the same with Mary. I wouldn't be invited for spook nights or to watch horror films. I'd find myself with no friends and be left out of all the fun times." I felt myself near tears when I admitted this and Selene reached over and put her hand over mine.

"Those times aren't any fun for you, are they?" she asked.

"You have to give people a chance," said Hermie. "They're often more willing to listen than you realize. You're imagining their response in addition to everything else."

"You don't know them," I said, and I knew that I sounded sulky.

Suddenly Selene stood up and stretched. "But first we have to let it all out," she said. "And that's what we're going to do. That's why I brought you up here where no one can hear you."

Panic gripped my insides. *Ohmigod*, I thought. *Nonna was wrong. These two have brought me up here to a place where no one can* hear *me.* The familiar feeling of fear begin to overtake me as my imagination ran riot and I imagined being left here or abducted. It must have shown on my face because Selene beckoned me to stand up with her. I didn't budge.

"That's it," she said. "*That's* the feeling, isn't it? The one you're feeling now that is eating you up, taking over your mind."

I felt confused. What was happening? "Yes. I feel scared. I . . . I suddenly don't know if I can trust you," I whispered.

Hermie offered his phone. "Call your mom or Nonna, if you like."

"No. I'm sure it's okay. I . . . I don't know why it is . . ." I started.

"So say it," said Selene.

"I feel scared," I said in a small voice.

"Louder. Come on, stand up and say it," said Selene as I stood to join her.

"I feel SCARED," I shouted.

"LOUDER," urged Hermie, who had also stood up with us. "It's okay. Let it out. You're safe here. The only scary thing here is that feeling inside of you. Throw it away."

"Yell as loud as you like," said Selene, and she threw her head back and shouted to the sky, "I FEEL SCARED!"

Hermie did the same. "I FEEL SCARED! Come on, now, Eve, let it out. All those feelings you've been holding inside at all those spook nights, all those times you couldn't sleep and felt you couldn't tell anyone. Let it all out."

I took a deep breath. It was true. I'd been holding it all in for months, for years, pushing what I really felt down inside. I threw my head back as Selene had done and yelled to the sky. "I FEEL SCARED! IIIIIIII FEE-EE-EEE-EEL SCARED." And then I yelled it a few more times for good luck. It felt strangely liberating.

"Great," said Selene. "Now let's scream." And to my astonishment she opened her mouth and screamed and screamed and *screamed*. I had to put my fingers in my ears.

Hermie grinned at me. "It only works if you really connect with whatever's been bugging you."

"Wow. What's been bugging her?" I asked.

Hermie laughed. "Oh, lots of stuff. She can get really emotional sometimes, but, come on now, your turn. Really go for it."

I closed my eyes and dug deep into all the times I'd felt I had to shut up, button it, hold it all in, deep into all the tension that coiled within my fear of the dark, my jealousy of being second at everything. And then I let it rip. "A . . . A . . . Aaaa . . . AARRGH! AAAAARRRRGH. AAAAAAAAAAAARRRRRGH!"

I don't know how long I went on, but all of a sudden there was no scream left. All the bad feelings had gone and the whole situation seemed really, *really* silly. Here I was on top of a hill with two very unusual people who were named after planets yelling my head off. I felt like laughing, so I did, so much in fact that it set Hermie and Selene off, and soon we were all laughing like we'd heard the funniest thing ever. Tears were flowing down Selene's cheeks she was laughing so hard.

When we all calmed down a bit, one of us would chuckle and set the others off again, and then we'd be quiet for a bit, then another little chuckle, and then it was all done. All done. And I felt tired enough to sleep for a week.

Chapter Twelve

Secrets Out

"I need to have a family conference," I said later that day when everyone was home. The decorators had gone and we were sitting around the dining table after supper.

"But there's something I want to watch on TV," said Adam.

"Five minutes," I said. "It's important."

Adam rolled his eyes but he stayed where he was.

Mom and Dad looked worried.

"You're not on drugs, are you, angel? Ohmigod . . ." said Mom.

"No, Mom! I am *not* on drugs. I am only twelve years old!"

"Kids start young these days," said Adam.

"Oh, shut up," I said. "And I'm not a kid."

"You've failed your finals?" said Dad.

"Let Evepud speak," said Lilith, who also looked worried. "She's got something serious to say and, for your information, we haven't had our finals yet, Dad."

It was time for my second secret to come out to my family. I took a deep breath and made myself remember all that Selene and Hermie had said. "Okay. I . . . I had my session with Miss Luna today and . . . I . . . oh . . ." There was only one way to do it. "A . . . A . . . AAAAARRGH! I AM AFRAID OF THE DARK!"

Mom looked alarmed by my outburst. "No need to shout, dear," she said.

"I AM AFRAID OF THE DARK!" I repeated.

"Ohmigod, she *is* on drugs," said Adam. "Classic symptom: can't gauge the volume of her own voice."

"No, Adam, I am not on drugs. I am scared of the dark."

"Since when? You're always up for spook nights . . ." he said.

"And scary movies . . ." said Lilith.

"I hate them. I've always hated them. They frighten me and give me nightmares."

"Spook nights? Scary movies?" Dad repeated. "Wha—"

"Since when, dear?" Mom interrupted.

"Since I was about six," I replied.

Adam looked shocked. "Seriously?" he asked.

"Seriously."

"No, I meant since when have you had these spook nights?" Mom asked.

"Oh . . ." I started. Lilith was looking at me intently and Adam looked worried. "I . . . it's a secret . . ."

Mom sighed and shook her head. "You girls and your secrets. I don't know . . ."

"Why didn't you ever say that you were scared of the dark?" asked Dad.

I glanced at Lilith. "I didn't want to be left out."

Mom got up, came over, and put her arms around me. "My poor baby. You could have told us."

"I thought you'd all think I was sissy or stupid."

"Well, you are," said Adam.

Lilith kicked his calf. "That's not very helpful."

Adam shrugged. "It is sissy, but it doesn't mean I don't care. You don't have to come anymore if you don't want to."

"But that's what I was worried about," I blurted. "That I'll be left out of the spook nights."

"What *exactly* are these spook nights you keep referring to?" asked Dad. Adam and Lilith immediately folded their arms as if by doing so they could keep our secret outings to themselves.

"Oh, just nights we tell ghost stories and stuff," said Lilith. "Nothing major." She got up to go.

"Sit back down right now, young lady," said Dad. "No one's leaving this table until we get to the bottom of this. Now then, is anyone going to tell me what's been going on?" He gave Adam a stern look.

Adam shrugged his shoulders. "Like Lilith said, Dad, no big deal, just some nights we used to sit around and tell ghost stories. Don't all kids do that?"

"Not in the cemetery they don't," I heard myself say.

"What! Which cemetery?" asked Mom.

"Er . . . the one next door to where we used to live," I said, and then cursed myself. I didn't mean to blurt it all out so quickly, but somehow I couldn't stop myself. It was as if my counseling session earlier had freed my tongue and words were rushing out like water through a broken dam. Hermie and Selene had said to give my family a chance to understand, but it didn't seem to be going as well as they had suggested.

Dad turned his gaze to Lilith. "Well?" he said. "Do you have anything to add to this conversation?"

Lilith looked down at the table. "Yeah, maybe a couple of times we went out, but . . ."

"At night?" asked Mom.

Lilith nodded and Mom gasped. "And where were your dad and I?"

"In bed," muttered Lilith.

"Ohmigod," said Mom, and she looked in horror at Dad, who shook his head. "Anything could have happened to you. You don't know who's going to be out and about late at night. I . . . I . . ."

"Now then, Marissa, keep calm," said Dad, although he looked far from calm himself. "All are present and accounted for. But I can tell you one thing, from now on we're going to be keeping a closer eye on what goes on in this house. And out. These spook nights are banned. And so are scary movies. And I would have credited all of you with more brains than to sit around telling ghost stories and scaring the life out of each other."

"It was fun," muttered Adam in hardly a whisper.

"What's that you said?" Dad demanded.

"Nothing."

"And Eve and Lilith, you can sleep in our room tonight because P. J. wants to get started on your rooms first thing. So, Eve, you needn't worry about the dark tonight. We'll be there. After that, well, we'll work on it together. And, Adam, I trust that you're old enough not to do anything this stupid ever again."

Adam and Lilith both glared at me. I glared back.

Later that night, we had a family TV night. We all watched the History Channel. A documentary about some ancient king. It was so boring. I tried to catch Adam's and Lilith's eye a couple of times so that I could make a funny face or something, but they wouldn't look at me. They sat stiffly with tight lips. I offered to make hot chocolate but only Mom and Dad wanted some. Later, Mom and Dad locked up and we trudged up to bed in silence.

This is exactly what I didn't want to happen, I thought as I went to brush my teeth. *Two secrets out and I've managed to upset everyone, and now Adam and Lilith hate me. Heaven knows what they'll make of my last secret.*

Chapter Thirteen

Second Zodiac Week

"When do you move back into your own room again?" asked Mary as we made our way onto the playground during lunch break the following Friday.

"Next week," I said, "P. J. said that my and Lilith's rooms are almost finished and I'm dreading it. Just thinking about it makes me feel tense."

"Okay," said Mary. "Maybe it's time to ask the zodiac people for help again. So, P. J. is also known as Pluto, and you think your counselor's name is something to do with the Moon?"

I nodded. "Yeah. Luna means Moon and Hermie is a nickname for Hermes, which is another word for Mercury. I looked it all up in a book about ancient gods in Dad's library."

"Wow," said Mary as we sat on a bench near the bike racks. "Let's see your phone again."

I sat next to her and passed her the phone. She glanced down at the list. "There are ten on here. You've met four. Nessa . . ."

"Venus; P. J., Pluto; Selene the Moon; and Hermie, Mercury."

"Okay, Eve, I think the explanation is simply that they all have nicknames. Have you called any of the other numbers on here?"

"Yeah. Dr. Cronus. He's a headmaster apparently. Sounds very strict."

"Why did you phone him?"

"I . . . er . . . I couldn't sleep when I got to the new house."

"Oh, yeah, that," said Mary matter-of-factly. "Lilith told me." She laughed. "She's mad at you, isn't she?"

I nodded. "It's weird. She's never been this angry at me before and I don't know if it's because I'm not going along with all her plans or because I'm a Zodiac Girl or because I told Mom and Dad about the spook nights."

I missed our twin closeness and the way we could almost read each other's minds. And there had only been a few times since I became a Zodiac Girl when we echoed what the other was saying. Normally that happened every day.

"Probably all three. She'll get over it. Why don't you call one of the other names on here? See what happens."

"I guess I could. Which one?"

Mary looked down at the list again. "Neptune.

Captain John Dory. Neptune rules the realm of dreams according to my astrology book. I remember because there was a picture of him in there dressed up as a king. King of the Sea."

"Maybe he could help with my nightmares," I said.

Mary handed me the phone. "Yeah. What have we got to lose?"

I pressed the button opposite his name and Mary put her head next to mine so she could listen, too. Moments later, a man with a gruff voice answered. "Hello?"

"Yeah. Hi. It's Eve Palumbo. P. J. gave me a phone with your number on it."

"Excellent. So you must be our Zodiac Girl."

"I am, and I wondered . . ."

"Do you like fish and chips?"

"Yeah."

"Live near Osbury, don't you?"

"Yeah."

"So come on in."

"Pardon?"

"Poseidon. Look for a fish-and-chips restaurant called Poseidon. That's me." And he clicked off.

"Yum," said Mary. "Let's go."

"Yeah. Let's go," I said. "I wanted to go by the village anyway to get a present for Lilith to try to make up for telling Mom and Dad about the spook nights."

"Good idea," said Mary. "You could get her something lovely like a skull or a Halloween mask."

We caught the bus that would have taken us home but got off a couple of stops early in the village of Osbury and soon found the fish-and-chips place in the main street of town. The door opened with a *ching* sound and the smell of frying and vinegar hit our noses, making my mouth water. On the wall opposite the door was a mosaic in green, gray, and blue. It depicted the King of the Sea with white hair and a big white beard holding a trident and sitting on a huge seashell. Around his feet were different species of fish in the waves. Behind the counter was a middle-aged man who looked exactly like the king in the mosaic— like he'd stepped out of the mosaic and come to life. He looked up at us and beamed. "Cod and chips twice and two Cokes?" he asked.

We nodded. *Bizarre*, I thought.

He served us two portions and indicated that we should sit at one of the tables opposite the counter. "Eat now, talk later."

We did as we were told and after we'd eaten and the Captain had served a few other customers he came over to join us.

"How's your zodiac time going, young lady?" he asked.

"Strange," I said.

"How far in are you?" he asked. "End of your second week, by my reckoning."

"I think so. P. J. said it was for a month."

"Can you help her?" asked Mary. "She has nightmares."

Captain John looked at me with blue eyes that twinkled like the sun on the sea. "Do you now?"

I nodded. "I'm scared of the dark, too, but I expect you know that already."

"I had heard," he chuckled. "I can tell you some secrets about dreams, though, and nightmares. You can train yourself to control them."

"No way," Mary and I chorused.

"Yes way," said Captain John. "Do you both have a television at home?"

"Yes," we chorused again.

"Use a remote?"

"Yes."

"And what do you do when there's a show on that you don't like?"

Sit through it, I thought, *because usually Adam or Lilith have the remote.*

"Change channels," Mary replied.

"Exactly," said the Captain. "It's the same sort of thing with your dreams. If you're having one you don't like, you mentally change channels. Go to something you'd rather see."

"No way. Could I really do that?" I asked.

"Absolutely. Takes some practice, but, yes, you could. Give it a try anyhow. Other thing you can do is think about nice things before you go to sleep because quite often what you've been thinking about comes up in your dreams, doesn't it? Fears, worries, anxieties— you have to replace them with happier thoughts."

"That's what Nessa said."

"She's right. Before you go to sleep, say to yourself: have good dreams, have good dreams. It programs your mind," said Captain John.

"No bad dreams, no bad dreams," I said.

The Captain shook his head. "No, don't say it like that. Don't emphasize the negative to the unconscious mind, only the positive. The unconscious doesn't hear the word no. So if you say, "No bad dreams, no bad dreams," it hears only "bad dreams." Put it in a positive way—"Have good dreams, have good dreams." You see the difference?"

"I think so," I said.

"So give it a try," said the Captain as another customer came in. "Good luck."

He got up to serve the new customer and we got out our purses to pay for the fish and chips. "On the house," he said.

"Sounds a bit too easy," I said when we got outside. "Thinking happy thoughts and telling yourself to have good dreams when you've got the heebie-jeebies is easier said than done."

"Worth a try, though," said Mary as we crossed the street and made our way over to the bus stop. "And . . . well, I just wanted to say something else, too. Next time you're feeling scared of the dark and can't sleep, you can always call me, you know, maybe not on the zodiac phone but on your normal cell phone. That's what friends are for."

Later that night, I snuggled in on the cot in Mom's room and thought about what Captain John had said about my nightmares. It would be amazing to be able to control them, especially as they were such a big part of my life, like a bad habit I couldn't kick. I got comfortable, and, as Nessa and Captain John had told me, tried to think about nice things. I imagined Captain John as the King of the Sea and Nessa as a goddess dressed in white dancing up in the clouds.

I drifted off to sleep without any problems. It was lovely: the King of the Sea with fish dancing around his feet, Nessa as a goddess by his side in a seashell. And then the seashell changed into a sled and the sea changed to snow. They were flying through fields of white toward some woods. It got dark as they approached the woods. Trees cast deep shadows. I couldn't see the sky anymore and the trees grew menacing, like skeletons with pointed bony hands.

The King of the Sea and Nessa seemed to be changing, their cloaks of white and blue were turning black. They weren't flying anymore. The ground was rough and it was difficult to see.

And suddenly I was in the cemetery. Nessa and Neptune were gone and in their places were figures in hooded cloaks. When I looked closer, they had no faces.

Change the channel, change the channel, I told myself. *Happy thoughts, happy thoughts.* The figures were coming toward me. A feeling of dread was welling up in my stomach. *Change the channel, change the channel, happy thoughts, HAPPY thoughts.* But it wasn't working. It was like pressing a remote that had a dead battery, and the hooded figures were getting closer.

I was so freaked out that I woke with a start to find that my heart was beating fast and I was hot. Across the room, I could make out the sleeping form of Lilith turned away from me toward the wall and, up on the bed, I could hear Dad's gentle snoring. *You're okay, Eve,* I told myself. *You're safe.* I threw off my covers for a second and cooled down, and a few moments later my heart began to slow. I snuggled back down. *I can do this,* I thought as I felt myself grow drowsy again. *I can do this, have good dreams, have good dreams.*

A short time later I was back in the woods, skeletons

of trees beckoning me forward. *Oh no, I don't like this,* I thought. *It's getting spooky.* And then there they were, the hooded figures coming closer. *No, no. Go away. I want to watch another channel. I can do it, too. Light and sunshine. Nice things. Think nice things, Eve.*

Candy. Er . . . strawberries and sunshine and picnics and people laughing. All of a sudden, the figures threw off their cloaks: they were fairies with strawberry-pink hair piled on top of their heads, wearing green tutus like strawberry leaves and rain boots. They began doing a funny stomping dance. And then someone poked me in the side.

"Eve, stop laughing," said Lilith.

"Wh-what?" I murmured.

"You were laughing in your sleep," she said. "Shut up."

"Sorry," I said, and snuggled down again. I couldn't wait to get back into my dream. It was like having my own Walt Disney movie inside my head.

Chapter Fourteen

Zodiac Week Three

"*I* want to make it for him," said Lilith when she realized that I was making coffee for P. J.

"But I promised *I* would," I said, "and he is *my* zodiac guardian."

"Yeah, but Nonna hired him for all of us," Lilith protested.

"Now, now, what's all the whining about?" asked Mom, coming in from the hall.

"Eve thinks she owns P. J.," said Lilith.

"I do not. I was just making coffee for him," I said.

"I'll make it," said Mom, "Get some of those lemon cookies that he likes from the cookie jar to have with it."

"Mom's got a cru-ush, Mom's got a cru-ush," I sang, and even Lilith had to smile as Mom blushed. When Dad came through in his usual morning rush a few moments later and looked at us all suspiciously, we collapsed with laughter.

"What is going on?" he asked.

Lilith and I went and put our arms around his waist

and gave him a hug. "Nothing," I said.

"Just talking about what a great dad we have," said Lilith.

And that made Mom, Lilith, and me crack up laughing again.

Dad grabbed a piece of toast from the plate on the table. "I will never *ever* understand women," he said. "See you all later."

As Mom started making coffee, my zodiac phone bleeped that I had a message.

Da Sun enters Scorpio on October tventy-third. Mr. Sonny O has sent you a geeft in celebration of dis. Venus is vell aspected dis veek and she, too, vill bestow a geeft on you. I am bringing dem vith me on Thursday. See you laters. P. J.

I smiled at the way he wrote and the way he spoke. At first I'd found it hard to understand him, but now I spoke P. J.-speak perfectly and found his funny accent charming. My feelings toward him had totally changed by week three of my time as a Zodiac Girl. In fact, I could no longer even imagine a time when I was scared of him. Now I looked forward to his arrival each morning and wanted to make his stay with us as enjoyable as possible.

P. J., Natalka, Oleksander, and their team of workers

had totally transformed the downstairs of the new house. The hall looked warm, welcoming, and modern in honey-gold colors with lovely cedar blinds on the windows. The living room was done in a deep red color that suited the Victorian style of the house, and P. J. had knocked the kitchen and dining room into one big open space at the back of the house. He had decorated it in a Moroccan style, using rich colors of ochre, orange, and deep red. It looked fabulously stylish.

P. J. liked to arrive before his team and have a chat about his ideas with everyone in the family, but he always made time to talk with me about anything that was troubling me. As the days went on, I began to feel more confident about dealing with my fears, and I was certainly sleeping better. I hadn't been alone in my own room, though, because P. J.'s team had been working in there. They had promised to get it ready in time for my and Lilith's birthday.

I had a second session with Selene (this time in a more official-looking place in Osbury) and she showed me more techniques for dealing with stress or fear. My favorite one was to close my eyes and imagine that I had a bunch of deflated balloons in my hand. Then I had to imagine blowing all my fears into the balloons and, when I'd used as many as I felt necessary and they were as full as they could be, I had to imagine releasing them into the air and watching them fly away. Goodbye, fears.

That Thursday evening, Lilith and I got home to find P. J. standing in the hall waiting for us with a pile of packages.

"Happy birthdays," he said and then pointed upstairs. "Ve are ready."

"Ohmigod," said Lilith. "Our rooms?"

P. J. nodded. "And presents from da planets for Eve—I have three geefts for you: one from Mr. O, he is da Sun, and two from Nessa, who you know."

I noticed that Lilith's face dropped slightly when she heard this and I was so sorry for her. I really felt bad when I got stuff and she didn't.

"And, Lilith," said P. J., "I have two geefts for you, too. I not forgettings dat dis is your birthday, too. I hope you like dem."

Lilith's face lit up again.

"But first ve are showings da rooms," he said as he beckoned us to follow him up the stairs.

"Okay, first lady," he said when we reached the upstairs hallway. "If okay vith you, Eve, ve showings Lilith first?" And he gave me a conspiratorial wink.

"Absolutely," I said. "It's only fair. She was the first twin."

And I meant it. I didn't feel bad at all about Lilith going first because I knew that my turn would come. This was definitely something I wasn't going to be left out of.

"Okay, closing eyes," he said.

We closed our eyes and heard him open the door, and then he ushered us in.

"Okay, opening eyes," he said.

"Wow!" we chorused when we looked around the room. "It's gorgeous."

It was, too. It was a goth girl's dream. Three walls were painted matt black as Lilith had wanted and the fourth one was a deep crimson. Against this was a four-poster bed with a canopy of black lace. Across the bed was a black silk bedspread with crimson cushions and propped up against it was a Victorian porcelain doll. I'd never seen anything so romantic in my life and it wasn't spooky-looking at all.

"Ohmigod, I love it," said Lilith as she went over to the black lacquered dressing table to the right of the bed. On it was a silver vase filled with dried red roses and a wrought-iron candelabra. "This is the best birthday present ever. It's all . . . perfect."

"And look, Lilith," I said as I turned and saw the long mirror that looked as if it had been rescued from some ancient castle somewhere. "It looks so old."

Lilith gave P. J. a hug. "You are a total star," she said.

He smiled back at her. "Not exactly, but almost. And now, Eve. Ready for your turn?"

I nodded. I couldn't wait to see what he'd done with mine. As before, we were told to close our eyes and

P. J. guided us across the hallway and into my room.

"Opening eyes now," said P. J.

"Ohmigod!" we chorused again and smiled at each other when we realized that we were once more in sync after weeks of feeling apart.

My room wasn't that different from Lilith's, only it was pink. Three walls were painted in a pale pink, the fourth in a deep fuschia color that had a satin sheen to it. On the right edge of that wall was a scattering of tiny silver butterflies, hundreds of them, flying up to the top of the wall and dispersing as they flew across. While Lilith's furniture was black lacquer, mine was all silver. And I also had a four-poster bed. It had a canopy of pink lace cascading down, and tiny silver butterflies had been sewn into it to match the ones on the wall. It was divine.

"My room is goth princess," said Lilith. "Yours is fairy princess."

"Do you like it?" asked P. J.

"Oh *yes*," I said. I'd been worried that it might look a little sugary, but it didn't at all. It looked bright and fun.

"Okay, and here are your birthday geefts," said P. J. "Some for Lilith and some for Eve."

Lilith unwrapped hers first. One was a thick notepad with a black velvet cover and red spiral binding down the spine. Her second present was a fab red pen with a red feather.

"Dese are for writing your goth poetry in," said P. J.

For a brief second, Lilith looked sheepish. "Oh thanks. I, er . . . I usually write my poetry straight onto the computer," she said.

"I know," said P. J. "Why not try writing in da book next time?" And he gave her a pointed look that made her blush even more.

Something is going on here, I thought as I watched them. *Something to do with her poetry. Lilith rarely blushes.* As P. J. watched me unwrap my gifts, I made a mental note to ask her later.

The first gift was a poster from Nessa and it came with a note. It was of a beautiful woman dressed in a Grecian robe with a bow in her hand. She also looked remarkably like Selene.

"Artemis," said P. J. "Goddess of light. She is also known as da huntress. Just da thing to have on your bedroom wall if you don't like da dark, don't you think? She'll chase off anything you don't like vith her bow and arrow."

I nodded but for a brief second, when I imagined myself all alone in my gorgeous pink room, I felt the old familiar welling up of fear. I quickly pushed it down.

My second present from Nessa was a little bottle of essential oil. I took off the top and sniffed. "Lavender," I said. "I know because we had some in the backyard of our last house."

P. J. nodded. "And da best oil to help you sleep. Sprinkle some on your pillow. It's vot dey used to do in France in da old days. In fact, dey used to sew lavender bags into pillows to help sleep."

"Cool," said Lilith. "I might do that, too."

"Unwrap da last von," P. J. instructed. "It's from Mr. O."

I did as I was told and saw that it also came with a card. I opened it up and read out loud what he'd written: "Darkness is merely the absence of light. Love Mr. O XXXX. Where there is light, there can be no darkness."

I opened the box. It was a tiny lamp. I plugged it in and it cast a soft pink glow into the room.

"I don't know why you didn't think of having a nightlight before," said Lilith.

"Because I was too scared to speak up for what I wanted and too ashamed you'd think I was a sissy," I replied.

Lilith gave me a hug. "So, Evepud, you going to be okay now?"

I nodded. A small lamp with a soft bulb would be perfect! It wasn't too bright to keep me awake, but bright enough to keep my fears at bay. With my pink room, my huntress goddess looking over me, and my new lamp, the shadows that the dark brought were fast receding.

Chapter Fifteen

Zodiac Week Four

My pink room was a success.

My little lamp was a success.

My getting-to-sleep techniques were a supersonic-fabbie-dabbie-doobie success. By the end of my fourth week as a Zodiac Girl, I felt like a new girl. I was sleeping happily in my own bed in my own room, by myself. I felt stronger, more like my own person—like I'd gotten it sorted out and there was nothing more to fear. P. J. and his team had done the bathroom (lovely sand and sea colors), Adam's room (blue and charcoal—he likes it!), and were finishing off Mom and Dad's room.

"So I guess that's it, right, P. J.?" I said as he got ready to go on the evening of October 31. "End of my time as a Zodiac Girl?"

P. J. shrugged. "Not quite. It is alvays up to each Zodiac Girl to make of her time vot she vill. Some resist. Some ignore. I am thinking you have made good efforts. You are feeling better, *ja*?"

"*Ja*," I said, and I held out my hands to display my

newly manicured nails. I'd had them done at the Pentangle salon yesterday after school, and it was the first time in years they weren't bitten down and raggedy.

P. J. smiled. "*Ja*. Dis is good. Only one last thing. Saturn is square to your Sun in da last veek . . ."

"Vich means vot?" I asked.

"Vot you make of it. Saturn is da taskmaster of da Zodiac—"

"Dr. Cronus?"

"*Ja*. Dis is da planet dat teaches you big life lessons. If you have learned your lessons, it vill be easy peasy lemon squeezies; if you resist lessons, oooh, it can be difficult."

"No probs," I said. "I haven't resisted anyone. I feel like a totally new person."

"*Ja*, no probs," said P. J., but he looked at me with concern for a moment and my newfound confidence buckled just for a second.

The talk at school all week had been about Halloween, with people making masks in art class, writing ghost stories in English, discussing the origins of the night in history. Of course Lilith was working hard on a Halloween poem, spending hours on the computer and not letting anyone see what she'd written until she'd finished. I wondered if maybe it was time to let my third and final secret out.

When it came to the night of October 31, Lilith came

down in her Halloween costume. It was a skeleton outfit, which consisted of old black leggings, a black T-shirt, and a black stocking with a nose cut out which she'd pulled over her face. She'd painted on white bones and a skull in glow-in-the-dark paint. It was really effective when we turned off the lights. Mary was dressed as a witch in a black dress, and she'd painted her face green. Adam had a matted gray wig on, tattered clothes, and bits of gloop hanging off his skin.

"What are you supposed to be?" I asked. "You look like you've just crawled out of a vat of porridge."

He looked at me with indignation. "A zombie," he said.

"No change there, then," I said, and gave him a snide grin.

This year, he was going to a high school party with his friends, so he wouldn't be going trick-or-treating. Judging from the overwhelming amount of aftershave he was wearing, I thought he was hoping to get lucky with some girl.

"Hadn't you better hurry up and change, Eve?" asked Mary after Adam had gone.

"Yeah," said Lilith. "We've only got a few minutes before we're supposed to join the other trick-or-treaters and Miss Regan from our school. "You're not even dressed yet."

"I'm, um . . . not coming this year," I said.

Lilith look surprised. "Why not? Oh. Is it because you're still scared of the dark?"

I shook my head. I knew that I had to say what I felt and my weeks as a Zodiac Girl had given me the courage to do it. "Not really. More because I feel that I've grown out of it—like roaming the streets with a bunch of people dressed as zombies, devils, witches, and vampires just isn't my thing. It never really was."

"Oh," said Lilith. She looked disappointed, but she didn't argue.

"And, um . . . also, Nessa said she'd come over and cut my and Mom's hair," I said.

Lilith raised an eyebrow. "Nessa from Pentangle?" she asked.

I nodded and I could see that Mary looked torn between going out into a cold rainy night and staying in for a girls' evening. She ran her hand through her hair. "I could use a trim, too."

"Don't you *dare* abandon me, Mary," said Lilith. "You *promised* and you've already got your costume on."

Mary shrugged. "Okay, okay, but we don't have to stay out too late, do we?"

Lilith shrugged her shoulders. "I don't know what's happening to everyone around here anymore. Like, where did all the fun go? And what happened to our traditional Palumbo spook night on Halloween?" She stomped out.

Mary whispered to me, "Maybe what we used to think of as fun has changed and you're the only one with enough of a brain to realize it." But she followed Lilith out of the room anyway.

"I guess," I said. It felt good to accept that Lilith and I had some things that we'd always do together, but we could also do things separately.

Mom and I had a cozy night in with Nessa, and Nonna showed up halfway through the evening, bringing a big yummy box of Belgian truffles with her. *Now this is my idea of a good night*, I thought as we listened to music on the CD, stuffed our faces with chocolate, and flipped through magazines looking for hairstyles. I'd never had an evening like this with my mom before, but she seemed to be enjoying it as much as I was. Nessa cut Mom's long straggly hair to her shoulders and showed her how to apply a little make-up. It was a hundred percent improvement. She looked really beautiful and lots younger. When it was my turn, she cut my hair a little shorter, put some layers in, and cut bangs. But, best of all, she put in bright pink highlights. It looked fantastic. When Dad came home, we asked if he'd like a trim, too, but he ran and hid in the kitchen. Nonna thought it was hilarious and couldn't stop laughing. *Just as some things will change, I also have to accept that there are certain things that never will*, I thought. *And Dad's scruffy style is one of them.*

After Nessa left, Nonna and I settled down in front

of the TV with a bowl of popcorn to watch a romantic comedy. Mom and Dad popped out to pick up Adam from his party. Nonna soon dozed off and didn't even stir when my normal cell phone rang.

It was Mary. She sounded out of breath. "Eve, you have to come. L-Lilith's in trouble."

"Yeah, yeah," I said. "You don't fool me that easily."

"No really, Eve, please come. I'm really scared for her."

"Halloween set-up. Yeah, yeah. Tell you what. You and she can come home now. In fact, it is getting a bit late."

"I know. I *really* want to come back but . . . *please*, Eve, you have to believe me! This *isn't* a joke. I promise you."

She did sound freaked out and I began to wonder if something really was amiss. "Where are you?"

"In the cemetery and Lilith's in—"

"Next to our old house?"

"Yeah."

My heart sank. "Oh, come *on*, Mary. Now I know it's a set-up. Lilith was annoyed that I didn't want to come out with you tonight for a spook night and now she wants to get me down there and scare me. No. I'm through with all that."

"No, *no*, really." Mary's voice wobbled. If she was acting, then she was doing a very good job of it. "Please come quick. I'm really scared."

"Mary? What's happened? Why should I go down there if it's not for them to try to spook me?"

"I can hear her calling, but I don't know where she is. Ohmigod, Eve . . . I have to go. Someone's coming. Come quick, *quick*."

The line went dead. I immediately tried to call back, but it went straight to voicemail.

I glanced over at Nonna, who was still sleeping soundly. I wondered whether to wake her. A feeling in my gut told me that Mary wasn't kidding around. Lilith was in trouble. It was a twin thing. I could always sense when something was seriously wrong with her—like the time she fell and broke her wrist when we were seven and the time she was in a car accident and bumped her head. *Now what have I learned from P. J. and the zodiac people?* I asked myself. *Ask for help, and darkness is only the absence of light.*

I went to find the biggest flashlight we had in the house and then I stuffed my zodiac and other phone into my pocket and called Mom's cell phone from our land line. A second later, it rang from where she'd left it, on the kitchen table. Next to it was Dad's. *Typical*, I thought. They never took their phones with them anywhere.

I went back into the living room, gently woke Nonna, and filled her in on Mary's call. She leaped up immediately. "I'll phone for the car," she said.

"Okay, but I'm going to find Lilith," I said.

"No," said Nonna. "We'll go together. Wait for the car."

I nodded, but when Nonna went up to use the bathroom, as I waited at the foot of the stairs, I swear

I could hear Lilith calling for me. It was faint, like a wisp of smoke in the back of my mind, but there it was again and . . . I swear she was saying . . . *Oh no!* She was in the crypt! *No. Noooo. She couldn't be. She wouldn't have been that stupid, would she?* I asked myself.

I couldn't wait for the car. I scribbled a note for Nonna—*Gone to Grebe Street, cemetery, maybe crypt, see you there as soon as possible*—and left it on the hall table where she'd see it when she came down. I opened the front door and slipped out into the night. It was dark and stormy outside. The wind howled through the trees, causing them to bend and sway. Up in the sky was a full Moon like a huge white specter looming over the streets and houses. *Lilith Palumbo, I am going to kill you for this*, I thought as I pulled my coat tight around myself. *Unless you're already dead!* said a voice in the back of my head, causing me to shudder.

Out on the sidewalk, there were still people around—stragglers from trick-or-treating, older teens on their way to parties. At least, I *hoped* they were trick-or-treaters or partygoers—a posse of white-faced witches cackled at me. A group of zombies limped past and leered. A vampire ran up to me, his cape blowing in the wind. At least *he* didn't scare me. He was only three feet tall and about six years old!

"Turn off the flashlight," someone shouted from farther down the street. "This *is* Halloween."

"So?" I said back in the direction of the voice. "Who says we have to stumble around in the dark?"

"The light is for the living, the dark is for the de-e-ead," said someone in a spooky voice behind me. I swung the flashlight around and saw that it was a fourteen-year-old boy from our street.

"Killjoy," he said. "Turn the fricking light off."

I took ignored him and ran along the sidewalk until I reached the road where our old house was. The SOLD sign was still up and there were no lights on so, hoping that the new owners hadn't moved in yet, I took the shortcut down by the side of the house into the backyard and through the hedges.

And there I was back in the very place I'd sworn never to return to. The cemetery. I'd been so mad at Lilith as I ran there that I hadn't had time to be too scared, but as soon as I found myself in that familiar territory all the old feelings came back, too. I shone the flashlight around, highlighting graves and shrubs. Something moved behind me, the snap of a twig, footsteps, as a shadow moved out from behind a shrub. I almost jumped out of my skin as I spun around with the flashlight.

"It's only me, Eve," said Mary.

"Waaaargh! You . . . almost . . . gave me a heart attack," I panted as I hugged her. "Where's Lilith? Have you found her?"

Mary pointed over toward the crypt. "I . . . I think

she's in there."

"Ohmigod, no! I *did* hear her. In the crypt! Is she out of her mind? No one goes in there. What happened? How did she get in there?"

"And she's not alone," said Mary as she pulled on my arm and we hurried past gravestones toward the crypt.

"What! Who's she with?"

"A bunch of kids."

"Nooo. Oh no. How many?"

"Five."

"Five? So that means that with Lilith there are . . ."

"Six," Mary finished for me, and I knew she was thinking of the same story I was. Six was the number of children who had been in there the night of the disappearance so many years ago. Six was the number of graves around the crypt. Six children whose remains were never found.

"But . . . how come?"

"We were going around trick-or-treating and one of the kids said it was too tame and that he wanted to get really scared and—"

"Lilith offered to show him this place?"

"Exactly. We broke off from the teachers and the school group and escaped in here. At first, it was all good fun and games until the same kid asked about the crypt and accused Lilith of being chicken and scared."

I could just see the scene. "And course she had to

show him that she wasn't."

"Right," said Mary. "We didn't even think it would be open, but the door was ajar and Lilith led them in there. I don't know what happened. The door shut behind them just as I got there. They're locked in and I can't get them out. I've tried and, ohmigod, Eve, what are we going to do? The kids are hysterical. Even Lilith is losing it. I've been out on the street looking for help. Anyone. Some adult. All the kids I've stopped are like you: they just think I'm doing a trick—you know, Halloween, locked in a crypt."

As we got closer, above the howling wind, I could make out another sound—the wail of howling kids.

"Lilith, *Lilith*," I called.

"Eve. EVE," I heard Lilith call back.

In seconds we were at the crypt, and the ten-foot metal door loomed in front of me, the wrought iron gleaming in the light of the flashlight. I pushed with all my might on it, but Mary was right: it was shut fast.

"Lilith, Lilith, I'm here," I said.

At the sound of my voice, the kids in there started howling louder. "Who's that?" one young voice cried. "Ith it a ghost?"

"It's my sister," said Lilith. "She's come to rescue us. Eve, get us out," Lilith called back. "I don't like it in here."

Mary and I tried shoving the door again, but it was no use. It was as solid as concrete.

"Lilith, we have to get the cemetery attendant," I called.

"But he'll kill us," she said, and the kids started wailing louder than ever. "Oh, for heaven's sake, SHUT up. I don't mean he'll *kill us* kill us, I mean he'll be mad. Angry." Her words didn't seem to be reassuring them and their howls grew louder.

I made myself calm down. "Is it dark in there?"

"Yes," said one of the kids.

I shone the flashlight under the door.

"I can see light," said Lilith. "Have you brought a flashlight?"

"Yes, and I . . ." I spotted a gap in the bottom of the door where the metal had rusted away. It was just big enough to poke the flashlight through. I took a deep breath. It meant that Mary and I would be out in the dark, but I knew how those children felt and I didn't want them to feel it a moment longer than necessary.

"Darkness is only the absence of light," I called. "Nothing to be frightened of." I pushed the flashlight through.

Next I pulled out my phone and called Nonna.

"Where are you, you bad, *bad* girl?" she asked.

"I'm sorry, Nonna, I had to go. I'm at the crypt in the cemetery. Lilith's locked in with a bunch of children. We can't open the door. Can you get help? Call Miss Regan—she's the teacher from our school who was overseeing the trick-or-treaters. She'll know who to contact."

"Right," said Nonna. "I'm on it. And call P. J. He can get in anywhere."

I pulled out my zodiac phone and pressed the button next to P. J.'s name. No sooner had I pressed it than he appeared from behind a gravestone of an avenging angel, causing Mary and me to almost jump out of our skins.

"You is calling me?"

"Yes. How? Whaa . . . ?"

He pointed over toward the back of the cemetery. "I live over dere. I often take dis route through da cemetery. It is a short cut. I saw you here before once, before you moved. *Ja.*"

"*Ja.*" *So it was him that I saw the last time I came here*, I thought. *I wasn't crazy.* "P. J., Lilith's locked in the crypt."

"I vas coming. I could hear howling," he said, and he ran his hand over the edge of the door. "First I thought it was da vind, den I realize it's people."

"Can you do anything? If they're still in there at midnight, they will turn to dust."

P. J. burst out laughing. "Who told you dis?"

"Everyone around here knows it," said Mary. "It happened to six children a couple of centuries ago."

"No, dis is not true," said P. J. "Dey vent home, to sleep in der safe own beds. Dey left der costumes in da crypt. Dat vas all."

"How do you know?" I asked.

"I voz here. I told you, I live across da vay in a basement apartment."

I shook my head. "That would make you ancient. You're as whacked as Lilith. But never mind that for now. Can you get them out?"

P. J. felt around in his pocket and pulled out an enormous key ring on which were about a hundred keys of all shapes and sizes. He began to try them one by one in the lock.

"Who's there?" Lilith called when she heard his fumblings.

"P. J.," I said. "It's going to be okay."

Moments later, P. J. found a key that fit, the door was opened, and the kids burst out, followed by a very shaken-looking Lilith. She was still in her skeleton costume but had taken the mask off. She was shivering with the cold, as were the children.

"It was . . . brr . . . brr . . . like a fridge in there," said Lilith.

One of the children screamed when she saw me and pointed from me to Lilith. "She's evil. She's made two of herself and now she's going to EAT us."

I almost laughed and would have if I hadn't seen that the little girl really believed it. I dropped down on my knee so that we were eye to eye. "She's not evil. She's my twin. You know what twins are, don't you?"

The girl looked from me to Lilith and back again, then nodded. "We've got twins at our school."

I gave her a hug and she clung to my neck like I was her long-lost best friend. "It's okay," I said. "You're okay and there's nothing to be afraid of."

Over her shoulder, I could see P. J., and he smiled down at me and nodded.

Mary gave the other children a big hug each and they hung around her legs, which was a strange sight because she was still dressed as a witch and most of the children were dressed as goblins.

"Now, all hold hands and ve're going to go to da gate," P. J. instructed.

Six little pale faces looked up at him.

"Good costume," a little girl remarked.

"Are you Dracula?" asked one little boy.

"No, not Dracula. Vhy is everyvon always saying dis? I am Lord of the Undervorld, Pluto, the great transformer, son of Ceres," he replied. "Who are you?"

"Kevin Patterson, son of Betty," the boy replied. "How old are you?"

"Four billion five hundred and forty-three years, three months, two days, five minutes, and twenty-two seconds . . . ish," he replied.

"Awesome," said the boy.

"Vhy? How old are you?" asked P. J.

"Six years, three months, er . . . three days, er . . . and not sure," said Kevin.

"Awesome," said P. J., and held out his hand. Kevin took it, and, solemnly and silently, the others joined hands and we began to walk toward the gate, Lilith showing the way with the flashlight.

"You okay?" I asked.

She shook her head and looked near tears. "Not really. I can honestly say that I've never been more scared in my life. It was really horrible in there, so cold, and we couldn't see anything. It was really spooky."

I took my coat off and insisted she put it on. She shook her head at first. "No, it's cold out here," she said.

"I know, but I haven't been locked in a fridge for over an hour. You wear it. I'll be fine."

She put it on and we put our arms around each other. "You're okay now," I said, and she leaned her head on my shoulder.

Suddenly, she gripped my arm. "Oh no, *nooooo*," she groaned. She pointed ahead toward the gates, fear distorting her face.

I looked up to see what she'd seen.

"Ohmigod," I gasped. It was a truly frightening sight. Not zombies or vampires or witches or goblins.

It was much, *much* worse.

It was a posse of angry-looking parents. And they were coming right at us.

Chapter Sixteen

Last Secrets

"Which one is Lilith?" asked one irate father as he scanned the strange-looking group standing at the cemetery gates.

Miss Regan had arrived, and Nonna with the car and chauffeur.

The children pointed in my and Lilith's direction. Lilith looked petrified, so I didn't hesitate for a second. "I am," I said, and I stepped forward.

Nonna was watching and I thought for a second that she was going to give me away, but I saw her glance at Lilith and I knew she understood why I was doing it.

"You'll pay for this," said the angry father.

"Yes. What on earth did you think you were doing?" asked a frazzled-looking mother whose child was wrapped around her neck, clinging on for dear life.

"I am really, *really* sorry," I said. "It was unbelievably stupid of me and I swear I will never ever do anything like that again. Please believe me."

"She ought to be given detention for the rest of

the year," said the father.

"She will be punished," said Miss Regan, stepping forward, "but for now let's get these children safely home to a warm bed. The school will decide how to deal with Lilith later."

Luckily the crowd was as anxious as we were to get home, and it quickly dispersed.

Soon after, we were in the back of Nonna's car on our way to our house. Lilith was very quiet and sat with her hands together, looking out the window. I took one of her hands in mine and she turned and smiled sadly.

Nonna was wonderful. She didn't say anything to Lilith, nor did she mention anything to Mom and Dad when they got back ten minutes after we did.

"Our little secret," she said when they went to hang up their coats. Then she ran a hot bubble bath for Lilith and made us hot chocolate, which she brought up into my room.

"Why don't you sleep in here with Eve tonight?" she said to Lilith when we'd drained our mugs. "You've had a fright."

Lilith looked at me. "Would that be all right, Evepud?"

"Of course," I replied. "Any time."

Mom set up the cot for her on the other side of my room and stood at the door smiling. "You girls, first you want your own rooms and now you want to be together."

"Only for tonight," said Lilith, "seeing as it's Halloween."

Later, when the lights were out, I sat up and turned my nightlight on. "Do you think you might write one of your poems about tonight?"

Lilith didn't answer for a while. "Actually, Eve, I . . . I have something to tell you about that. A . . . sort of secret . . ."

Now was the time, I thought. *I have to tell her my last secret.* "Me, too."

"Promise you won't hate me," we chorused.

"Promise," we said in unison again, then we both laughed.

"You go first," we both said, then laughed again.

"Okay," said Lilith. "I usually do, being the first woman and all."

"Exactly," I said.

"Here goes," said Lilith. "I . . . it's . . . ohmigod, this is hard. Okay, I'm just going to say it. You know my poetry? Well I don't write it. I get it from an Internet site that writes poetry for you. It gives you options, like you pick a line out of four and you just choose another one then another one and it puts it together, so you see I am a rotten cheat and don't deserve any of the prizes I've won and I bet you hate me now and think I'm worthless."

"I . . ." I didn't know what to say. Lilith hadn't

written any of her poems. "Not one of them? You haven't written one of them?"

"No. I am horrible at writing poetry. Totally awful."

"I . . . I . . ." I started to laugh. All that angst, all those spooky lines, she hadn't written any of them. She laughed a little, too, but I could tell that her laughter was more nervous.

"You won't tell anyone, will you?" she asked.

"Not if you don't want me to."

"I won't do it again. It didn't make me feel very good, being a cheat."

"I won't tell. Don't worry."

Outside, there was a flash of lightning that lit up our room followed by a deep rumble of thunder. It made both of us jump and Lilith looked particularly alarmed.

"Do you think that is a sign I ought to give my poetry prizes back?" she asked.

"Maybe," I said. "Or maybe it's just thunder."

A second bolt of lightning flashed and an even deeper rumble of thunder boomed over us. It sounded like it was right over the house.

"I . . . I think I should give the prizes back," said Lilith. "Yes. I will. I should."

"Your decision," I said. "I won't tell anyone."

We both lay and looked up at the ceiling.

"What's your secret?" asked Lilith after a few moments.

"I do write my own poetry," I said. "I have for years. I don't know if it's any good but . . . but it's not goth poetry, it's . . . about nice things, everything I like, including kittens. Promise you won't vomit."

"I promise," said Lilith.

"That's what I kept in my secret tin," I said, "along with the secret plans for my room."

Again, we were both quiet for a few moments while we digested the secrets that we'd told each other.

"For twins, we haven't done a very good job of knowing what the other one is thinking," said Lilith.

I thought back to how I'd heard her call from the crypt. "Sometimes we have. I think we will when we need to."

"Maybe," said Lilith.

"Definitely. We will always be twins. No one can ever take that away, but one thing has changed. I used to think that I am me but there are two of me. Now I think I am a twin, but I'm also a separate and unique person."

"Me, too," said Lilith.

And then we both burst out laughing.

The Scorpio Files

Characteristics, Facts, and Fun

October 24–November 22

Deep, mysterious, and passionate, Scorpios are great at keeping secrets. They are ambitious and determined and will do whatever it takes to get what they want, so don't stand in their way!

Although they love mystery and secrets, Scorpios hate being lied to and can be very suspicious. Be prepared for lots of questions and tantrums until they discover the truth!

Element:	Water
Color:	Black, dark red
Birthstone:	Opal, golden topaz
Animal:	Tiger
Lucky day:	Tuesday
Planet:	Ruled by Pluto

A Scorpio's best friends are likely to be:
Cancer
Pisces

A Scorpio's enemies are likely to be:
Aquarius
Taurus
Leo

A Scorpio's idea of heaven would be:
Being the detective on a murder-mystery weekend.

A Scorpio would go crazy if:
There was a secret and she wasn't let in on it.

Celebrity Scorpios

October 21 ✴ **Carrie Fisher**

October 24 ✴ **Kevin Kline**

October 26 ✴ **Hillary Clinton**

October 28 ✴ **Joaquin Phoenix**

October 28 ✴ **Julia Roberts**

October 29 ✴ **Winona Ryder**

October 30 ✴ **Henry Winkler**

November 2 ✴ **David Schwimmer**

November 4 ✴ **Sean Combs**

November 6 ✴ **Ethan Hawke**

November 7 ✴ **Joni Mitchell**

November 9   ✴   **Nick Lachey**

November 10   ✴   **Brittany Murphy**

November 11   ✴   **Leonardo DiCaprio**

November 13   ✴   **Whoopi Goldberg**

November 14   ✴   **Prince Charles**

November 17   ✴   **Martin Scorsese**

November 18   ✴   **Owen Wilson**

November 19   ✴   **Calvin Klein**

November 21   ✴   **Björk**

Eve's Top Tips for a Brilliant Bedroom Makeover

If repainting your whole room is out of the question, ask if you can paint just one wall. It will still make a huge difference to the room. Look for interesting paints—you can buy glitters, metallics, even magnetic types!

Changing the lighting in your room will make it look totally different. You could try twinkle lights, colored lampshades, or even candles, if you're super-careful with them!

Try pinning pieces of colorful fabric to the walls and

ceiling. They will make the room seem cozier, and it's much easier than putting up wallpaper!

Stencils are a cheap way to brighten up a plain wall. They are available at most craft stores and online.

Even if you're terrible at sewing, cushion covers are really easy to make and will make your room look great. Just fold some fabric you like into an envelope shape and sew down the sides.

Frame some pictures you like and ask an adult to put them up in your room for you. You could even paint the frames to match your color scheme!

Are you a typical Scorpio?

What's your best feature?
A) Your happy smile—you're always laughing.
B) Your shiny hair—straightened to perfection!
C) Your big eyes—dark and hypnotic.

You find out a big secret about someone you know. Who do you tell?
A) Anyone who'll listen! Secrets are meant to be told!
B) Only your best friend—she won't tell anyone.
C) No one. It's good to be mysterious, and it's not your secret to tell.

You and your friend both auditioned for the same part in the school play, but she got it. What do you do?
A) Congratulate her—she was obviously better than you for that part.
B) Grudgingly accept the role of understudy and hope she can't perform.
C) Never speak to her again—you're green with envy!

Your family wants to go on a ski trip, but you've never tried it before. How do you react?

A) You don't care, as long as it's a vacation!

B) Terrified—you're sure you'll break something.

C) Excited! You love a challenge, and skiing sounds like fun.

What's your favorite subject at school?

A) You hate them all—you'd rather be in bed!

B) Art—you like to let your creativity shine.

C) Gym—you're pretty competitive and you like to win.

You suspect that your best friend is hiding something from you. What do you do?

A) Who cares? It's probably not very interesting anyway . . .

B) Wait for her to tell you in her own time—you're sure she will eventually.

C) Throw a massive tantrum until she tells you. You're the only one allowed to have secrets!

How did you score?

Mostly As—slightly Scorpio

It sounds like you're not into secrets and mysteries. Let your Scorpio side shine . . .

Mostly Bs—sort of Scorpio

You have a very healthy dose of Scorpio personality!

Mostly Cs—super Scorpio

You're the dark and mysterious Scorpio people know and love!

Zodiac Girls by Cathy Hopkins

Every month a Zodiac Girl is chosen, and
for that month the planets give her advice.

Brat Princess
Leo

Bridesmaids' Club
Libra

Dancing Queen
Aries

Discount Diva
Taurus

Double Trouble
Scorpio

From Geek to Goddess
Gemini

Recipe for Rebellion
Sagittarius

Star Child
Virgo